TORMENT

A WHISKEY TANGO FOXTROT NOVEL

W.J. LUNDY

Illustrated by
HRISTO ARGIROV KOVATLIEV

Edited by
SARA JONES

TORMENT

A POST-APOCALYPTIC THRILLER

The Soldier: Book One
W.J Lundy

COPYRIGHT

AUTHOR'S NOTE

Torment is a story I first began writing in 2014 shortly after *WTF 5 Something to Fight For* was completed. I wanted to tell the story of how things unfolded back in the states and have it be a standalone book from the rest of the series. Because of the popularity of the primary story line, I kept shelving *Torment* and driving on with the *Whiskey Tango Foxtrot* primary band of characters. But then came *The Invasion Trilogy,* and then *Donovan's War. Torment* fell further and further down the to-do list.

Eventually, I adapted some of the early chapters of *Torment,* into a short story and released it with Amazon Publishing's Kindle Worlds under the title *Battle for Orchard Hill.* This was a decision I immediately regretted because I knew then that the story may never be completed. Then something happened; Kindle Worlds is gone, and with that, those chapters went back to the bench.

That motivated me to get back into the original manuscript and finish *Torment*, a story that I always enjoyed and thought needed to be told. *Torment* is not a rewrite of the Kindle Worlds novella, *Battle for Orchard hill*. *Torment* is the original imagining and telling of that story the way I always intended it to be.

If you read *The Battle for Orchard Hill* and gasped at the novella's ending, hungry for more, you will be happy to know that *Torment* is no short story—the content has tripled, the elements expanded and the heat turned up to high. *Torment* is now the book I always wanted it to be, and the first book of the *Soldier Series*, if the readers will it.

As always, thank you for reading, and I hope you enjoy ***Torment: A Post-Apocalyptic Thriller. The Soldier Book 1***

PROLOGUE

A PATH TO BATTLE

He was shocked awake, the sounds of mortar fire and machine guns, screams, and the blaring of sirens still ringing in his ears. His heart pounded and sweat rolled down his back. Hands balled into fists, he searched for his rifle in the bright moonlight that cut through the thin curtains. He swung his feet over the side of the bed, looking at the open window, struggling to clear the cobwebs from his head and remember where he was.

Slowly, his mind focused. He stared at the curtains swaying in a calm breeze. Outside, the distinctive calls of an owl replaced the sounds of fading mortar fire. This wasn't Iraq; he wasn't lying on an Army cot southwest of Fallujah. He was in a rented cabin near Tallulah Falls. He looked at the clock on the wall; it was just past 0400 hours.

Hanging his head, the soldier said to himself, "It's not a nightmare. To me, it's real."

"Decompression Syndrome" he called it—the effects of slamming on the brakes after running his life at terminal velocity for the last year. His brain was still catching up to his body. He just needed time to unwind the tight ball of wire he had wound up in his soul.

Knowing there would be no more sleep today, the man stood and stretched. A predawn hike through the woods would be good for him. He strolled across the cabin floor to the makeshift kitchen and turned on the coffee pot. Then he stepped out onto a covered front porch to consider the dark Georgia forest. Robert Gyles had been here for seven days, halfway through his two-week leave. When others opted to visit family or spend weeks on some tropical island, committing acts of debauchery, he chose the solitude of the forest.

Robert was at the end of his career. He'd spent plenty of post deployments doing crazy things, but this time he just wanted peace and quiet. After a year in Iraq, he'd come home to an empty apartment and news that his wife of four years had left him. Most of his belongings were gone and his credit cards all maxed out. While his buddies were headed off to Vegas, he couldn't find much to celebrate. So he unplugged, grabbed his fishing pole and backpack, and headed to the forest, a place he always felt at home. Two weeks of tranquility would do his brain some good before he had to get back to the base.

The coffee maker ended its symphony of popping and bubbling, and he turned to enter the cabin. Just as he stepped through the doorway, his phone ring. He stopped and stared at it. Only a handful of people knew the number. He'd just picked up the basic burner phone in a kiosk outside the post exchange days before this trip. The only people with his number were his soon-to-be ex-father-in-law and his command. The company was on block leave, with most of his command running a skeleton crew, so his heart skipped a beat, wondering what his father-in-law would want. Or maybe it was Tracy... maybe she was coming back.

He held the phone in his hand and studied the display while it continued to ring. He didn't recognize the number, but it was a Fort Stewart area code. His hopes vanished as he pressed the answer button and held the phone to his ear.

"This is Robert," he mumbled, already preparing to hear a story from one of his soldiers. It wouldn't be the first time he'd been bothered on leave to bail a Joe of out jail early in the morning.

"Sergeant Gyles?" The voice on the other end of the phone was apprehensive.

"Yeah, it's me."

"Sergeant, sorry to have to wake you so early in the morning in the middle of your leave. This is Lieutenant Michaels, platoon leader for Second Platoon, India Company."

"Michaels?" Gyles grumbled, moving across the room to fill a cup of coffee. "Where is Lieutenant Andrews?"

"He's checked out, Sergeant. Headed to Bragg. He

had orders to the Eighty-Second and wanted to add the block leave on top of his moving. Guess he was eager to get away from Stewart."

Gyles shook his head and took a sip of the hot coffee, remembering that Andrews was due to transfer out of the unit. "Okay sir, what can I do for you, LT?"

"We need you to report back to base, Sergeant—as soon as possible."

Sighing, Gyles took another sip. "Who screwed up this time? Was it Collier? That dumb animal."

"Screwed up?" Michaels asked.

"Hospital or jail? What did they do?"

"I don't understand, Sergeant... the battalion is being recalled. One hundred percent have been ordered to report back to base. There is a national emergency going on; haven't you been watching the news?"

"No, I'm on leave." Gyles groaned. "Must be some mistake. India Company is on block leave; we've got seven more days."

"I'm sorry. It's not a mistake. The entire battalion is on alert—well, the entire division, really."

"Wait, what the hell is going on? The entire division? Is it Korea? We've been through these alerts before and to be honest—"

"No, Sergeant, it's not an drill and it's not Korea. Something is happening here at home, a lot of lawlessness near the Capital. They are calling everyone in to provide riot control and humanitarian relief."

"That's not what we do," Gyles said. "That's a law

enforcement and National Guard mission. Let the Army Reserve deal with that shit." It wasn't normally his style to argue with or lecture officers, but it was early in the morning, and he was confused as hell.

"It's what we do now. We have a mission quickly spinning up. We need you back at Stewart ASAP. Call me at this number when you get in, and I'll brief you on everything."

"Now?" Gyles repeated, still in disbelief.

"We need you on the road. Call me when you get to the base, Sergeant."

CHAPTER ONE

DAY OF INFECTION PLUS SEVEN, 0300 HOURS

Hunter Army Airfield. Fort Stewart, Georgia.

Sergeant First Class Robert Gyles stepped off the back of the open-topped HMMWV—High Mobility Multipurpose Wheeled Vehicle—colloquially called the Humvee or Hummer by those who used them. At the edge of the airfield, he was surrounded by other soldiers, the troops leaving trucks and busses and scattering in all directions. The field was as busy as Times Square on New Year's Eve. Groups of uniformed men weighed down with gear quick-timed past him, searching for units of their own. He wore a heavy pack on his back and had a long rifle clipped to his chest; he was dressed for war. But that was not where he was going—at least he hoped not.

It was unseasonably cold for the time of year. He could see the condensation form on the exhale of every breath. He shook his head in frustration, thinking of the warm bed he could be in right now. An emergency phone call bringing him in was not what he wanted. And it was a vacation he really needed, a break after months in the desert. All he wanted was some fishing in the mountains. Gyles was a simple man... why was it so much trouble to disappear and be left alone for a week or two?

India Company was on block leave after having just returned from a twelve-month combat tour. The promise of a two-week leave was the only thing that had kept most of them hanging on over the final months of the deployment. Being back on an airfield after only seven days would be a kick in the balls to all of them. And why did it always have to be so damned early in the morning?

Gyles scanned the airfield, taken aback by the chaos. He'd seen full-blown drills in his career, but he had not seen this much activity since the division mobilized after 9/11. Something big was going on just miles away, and whatever it was had command on the edge of their seats. The old veteran missed most of the news. Between prepping his unit for block leave and dealing with family problems, he had intentionally tuned out while he was in the cabin.

His only current events updates were from the radio interruptions on his drive back to base. He heard the early news reports about the incidents in Europe and the Middle East. The broadcasters sent mixed messages, some calling it another terrorist attack, a new bioweapon making people crazy. Some news focused on the attacks; others, such as GNN, had blamed the military response for outbreaks of rioting and civil resistance. People were fleeing the violence in ways that rivaled the Syrian Civil War. Refugees were sick and trying to get across borders, while others fought for the last seats on aircrafts. With the spurs of panicked civilians, riots, and a fleeing public, the government was struggling to contain the chaos.

Early reports said the US borders were temporarily closed, conditions being evaluated daily. They said security was airtight, but activity was rising at open crossings as Human Rights groups attempted to smuggle in those stopped by the US Border Patrol. There were reports of violence along border regions in California, Arizona, and Texas. With many groups in full violation of immigration laws, martial law was instituted in several border cities between Mexico and the United States, and even along the Canadian border as rumors of rioting in Toronto spread.

As Gyles listened to the news, he figured command would just want to pull them back and go over contingencies. What else could they do? Military policing in the States was tricky business, and homeland defense was still one of their mission-critical tasks. But fighting illness and rioters wasn't their specialty. The National Guard had already mobilized, and this was really their job; India Company were hunter-killers, not police officers and riot control. He clenched his eyes tightly, trying to push off the thoughts of what was sure to be a massive headache.

"But, hey, it's good training, right?" he mumbled.

His men were the tip of the spear, and as much as it sucked to be standing in the cold, he would have been even more upset if his boys had been excluded. He stopped and stood his ground, watching large trucks of soldiers mustering at the end of a hangar bay. Everyone was rushing, always reactionary these days; never a step ahead.

Whatever, he thought, watching a flight of helicopters lift off. *But damn, things are moving fast.*

After only a week, this was soon. It usually took them weeks, or even months, to put an operation like this together. He was still surprised at the urgency, especially them demanding he drive through the day and night to report to duty.

"Why did I answer the damn phone?" he grunted.

Gyles rounded the corner, seeing a pair of Chinooks already spun up, turbines screaming over the early morning silence, rotating blades creating a storm of dust on the end of the flight line. He turned and spotted the rest of his men leaping from the canopy-covered transport trucks, the soldiers falling into columns with heads down, marching ahead the way he had done himself on dozens of drills before. Their efficiency made him smile. Even tired and pissed off, the sight of his men gave him strength. He took a deep breath; it was time to put on the game face. Even false motivation was better than no motivation.

Gyles spotted a lean and baby-faced-looking man in brand new camo. With the new guy was his recently assigned platoon leader—the same lieutenant who was lucky enough to make the call to cancel his leave and order that he report for duty. The babyface and LT were talking to his commanding officer. The man in charge spotted Gyles and waved him over. Gyles grimaced, watching the LT snap a stiff salute as the company commander dismissed him so he could speak to his platoon sergeant in private. They knew each other well and chewed a lot of the same dirt. Gyles had just completed a year in Iraq with the man, Captain Younger, who approached him and shook his hand.

"Kids," Younger said with a smile. "Catch me up, Sergeant. Tell me, how was your time off?"

Gyles shrugged. "I didn't catch many fish but filled the river bank with empty beer cans. Thanks for the recall, by the way."

Younger nodded, sensing the sarcasm. "Well, you can thank the President for that," the captain said, tightening his brow. "Listen, I need a good platoon sergeant out here today. Lieutenant Andrews already checked out and is on his way to Bragg, so you've got a replacement platoon leader." He paused and tossed a finger toward the young officer gathered feet away, staring intently at a folded map. "That's Lieutenant Michaels. He just arrived a few days ago. Wish you had more time to get to know each other before your first mission, but it's not going to happen. Listen, he's new, and he's as green as the Jolly Giant's balls, but he's good people."

"What about the doc?" Gyles asked. He'd heard

early rumors that a medical officer from the US Army Medical Command (MEDCOM) would be attached to his unit. He didn't know why, or what that meant for his mission.

"Well, just do what he says; he has command and control over this one."

"A doctor in charge? Who is he? Army?"

Younger frowned. "No, he's something different. His assignment orders came from MEDCOM, but he's not military. Best we could determine by looking at his papers, he's with the Public Health Services, loaned out from the Centers for Disease Control... part of their Epidemic Investigative Service."

"Like a medical spook. Sir, this just smells all kind of silly."

Laughing, the captain nodded his head. "That might be the understatement of the century. Now back to your lieutenant; he's new, and he's going to be counting on you."

Gyles struggled to hold back a smirk that was easily caught by Captain Younger. "Yeah, I spoke to Michaels briefly on the phone this morning after I arrived. FNG is an understatement ... is he even old enough to drink?"

Younger scowled. "I'd be lying if I said I'm happy about this. You know you'll be the one the men look to out there. LT has the platoon, but I'm depending on you. Shit, only half the company has shown up so far, and I don't know if we'll see any more. People are scared with the news coming in from overseas. I'm not bullshitting you right now—I need experienced leaders out there."

Gyles could see the concern in the man's eyes. "What's this all about, sir, sending me into the field blind with a green butter bar and some Fed doctor? You sure this is just a routine operation?"

Younger looked left and right then took a step closer. "It's not just you; it's all of us. By orders from POTUS, everything has been called up. Rumors are they've even floated the balloons and are pulling back all our overseas forces. Everything from Germany to Korea, including the guys in the sandbox. And to top it off, they are ordering all civilian aircraft be grounded until the crisis is over. Just tell me, how do I get my people home on leave when the airlines are all grounded?"

"I didn't know things were really that bad," Gyles said, suddenly regretting his vow to unplug from the news over the last week.

Younger laughed and tensed his jaw. "So far, it's been a classic clusterfuck. Hell, between you and me, I heard rumors that China has gone completely dark, a black hole. No word in or out in the last twenty-four hours."

"China dark?" Gyles again cursed himself for not listening more to the news on his drive out of the mountains, sticking to music stations and avoiding talk radio. "How the hell does that happen? What about the satellites? We've got to know something."

"Like I said, it's a clusterfuck. Brigade isn't happy,

either; that's for damn sure." Younger pursed his lips and looked up at the approaching junior officer. "Gyles, listen, they've tightened the ropes on your load-out. Light ammo and no ordnance. But I'm telling you right now, go with your gut. I don't care what some doctor says; protect your people. I need them all back here."

"Sir, what about the rest of the company? The battalion?" Gyles asked.

"D.C.," Younger said. "The Secretary of Defense wants the city surrounded and cordoned off. Any units not being sent to beef up the borders are going to D.C. We convoy out in a few hours. If you're back in time, you'll be rolling with us."

Gyles looked Younger in the eye. "All that fire-power in the Capital is going to piss people off."

"Already has." The Captain nodded. "Lots of reports of rioting and attacks against our advanced units."

Gyles looked down, not knowing how to respond. His people were trained to deal with civilians and had done well in Iraq. But these were Americans; he wasn't sure how his soldiers would respond.

The captain pointed to the two young men standing by. A uniformed man with no nametapes or patches, just shy of six feet, with shaggy hipster hair and deep-set eyes had moved in and was standing with Lieutenant Michaels. "Well, no time like the present. Let me introduce you to the new blood," Younger said.

The senior man waved them over, and like eager

students, the young officer and the doctor snapped and moved back into the circle. The captain made quick introductions before slapping Gyles on the back. "Bring 'em all home, Sergeant," he said, walking away and leaving Gyles alone with the new men. As soon as Younger left them, the officer turned and quick-stepped toward the helicopters with the doctor by his side.

Doctor Jeff Howard. Gyles did not know him but had been warned about him in the morning briefing. The man was nothing but eager and ready to prove his worth, even if it meant breaking a few hearts of those in his charge. Gyles had to grin, seeing the man's brand-new uniform without name tapes and freshly issued gear put together half-assed and backwards. He picked up his pace and walked to the left of the marching men.

He moved alongside Second Lieutenant Michaels, his new platoon leader, and asked, "Sir, you have everything you need?"

The officer looked back at him, nodding. "Sorry to call you in off leave, Sergeant. So, how are my men?"

"Locked, cocked, and ready to rock. Excuse me though, *L Tee*, but what's with the holdback on some of the gear? I read the loadout—my grenadiers are dry and no frags. What gives?" Gyles said, not missing the words of ownership the new officer placed on the platoon.

Doctor Howard stopped and turned to face him. "No, Sergeant—not today; none of that is necessary."

The young medical man stepped closer, his eyebrows furled in frustration. "We've been over this before. Command thinks—and, quite frankly, I must agree—this is a civilian interaction. There will be no need for any gun play. If there is violence, the state police can handle it. This is an escort mission only." He grinned and looked Gyles in the eyes. "I understand you have a combat patch on your right sleeve and feel that makes you a decision-maker, but not today, Sergeant. This is not Iraq. There will be no bravado in front of the medical team, got it?"

"Yes, sir." Gyles smirked and slowly dipped his chin. He looked away from Howard and turned back to Michaels, who'd stayed quiet during the outburst. "Sir, I haven't exactly been filled in on all of the details yet. But if this mission turns into what they say it could, we'll need full combat kits, not this augmented, amended shit they issued the men. What the hell is this all about, anyway?"

The officer held up a small, bound notebook. "Same as we last spoke on the phone; nothing's changed. We're just babysitters today. I know the threat assessment, and your concerns are noted. Majority opinion is we go in, grab the civilian medical staff, and head back. This isn't a combat mission."

Gyles shook his head. "Too easy," he said, thinking every time he's been told something is easy, it's not.

He turned to see the columns of soldiers approaching. Gyles pointed and directed the lieutenant forward, and together they fell in ahead of the pack, slowly moving among the men all armed to the teeth and weighed down with heavy packs. As the soldiers of India Company approached the waiting birds from the rear, Lieutenant Michaels began anxiously shouting last-minute instructions into the wind. With most of the veteran soldiers already wearing hearing protection, the LT's words literally fell on deaf ears.

Gyles put a hand on his young leader's shoulder, guiding him to the side near the ramp of the first Chinook as the others boarded. Howard looked back with an anxious expression. Gyles stepped off to the side to allow the marching men to pass by him. "Sir, they got it. We're ready."

"Roger that, Sergeant," the officer shouted back, his head nodding eagerly. "Make sure they all get on board. I'll be traveling in the second helo."

"Yes, sir." Gyles grimaced and watched him turn away, joining the rest of the men and disappearing into the tail end of the second helicopter.

"What's up with that, Sarnt? The green LT still being a pain in the ass?"

Gyles turned to see his leader of First Squad, Staff Sergeant Eric Weaver, pull in beside him. They had known each other a decade, both having checked in at Stewart together. They were in the same class when they earned their expert infantry badge and in the same company on the last deployment to Iraq. Equally qualified and with similar experiences, it was only by chance that Gyles was selected for promotions before Eric. Even though he technically was superior in rank,

Gyles still shared a close bond and friendship with his long-time battle buddy.

"Butter Bar needs to calm down. I'm worried the kid's going to burn himself out before we even get there," Gyles grunted.

"Don't worry, he'll relax once he busts his cherry; they all do." Weaver smiled, fishing a can of dip from a pocket on his sleeve. He slapped it against the heel of his palm before opening the can and stuffing a large plug under his lip. "So, what's really going on?"

Gyles shrugged, dipping his chin to the passing soldiers. "You've probably heard as much as me."

Weaver shook his head. "Don't mess with me, G-man. I ain't never heard of the Army sending two hookers filled with grunts to collect a medical team. Even in theater, we were never tasked with errands like this."

"It's all this rioting stuff and the illness at the borders making people crazy... got the brass all shook up. Guess these docs up in Virginia are experts or something. They specialize in vaccines."

"Whatever happened to buying a cat a plane ticket? You really need a private escort from America's best?" Weaver said.

"It is what it is, bro. Just do me a solid and keep your squad together. If what they're saying on the news is true, this op could become a lot more than an over-priced Uber lift," Gyles said. He reached out and put a hand on Weaver's shoulder then pointed to the squadrons of Black Hawks, prepped and spinning on the flight line. "I feel like we ain't being told something."

"Mushrooms, brother, fed full of shit and kept in the dark." Weaver laughed, moving away.

Gyles glanced up and caught a signal from the crew chief waving him forward. He turned and followed the last of the men onboard the CH-47. He dropped into a webbed seat just as the ramp closed.

The turbines increasing in pitch, the big machines defied gravity and lifted into the air. Gyles pushed back into the jump seat and let his eyes scan the red-lit compartment. His men sat back against the fuselage, packs between their knees and rifles held tight. Some slept while others nervously looked straight ahead. Toward the front, he saw Doctor Howard with maps pulled out over his lap and a green spiral notebook in his hand, feverishly taking notes.

He caught the smug expression of Weaver across from him. Gyles shook his head, waving off the man's sadistic grin. The helicopter bounced in turbulence and banked to the side. Gyles twisted and looked through a port window to see a full squadron of Black Hawk helicopters escorted by Apache gunships. He flipped his wrist and watched Weaver strain to follow his gaze.

"Da fuck?" Weaver yelled over the engine noise.

The crew chief, a stocky man with silver hair, a thick mustache, and wearing a green jumpsuit, moved closer. He knelt close so they could hear over the roaring of the Chinook. Gyles saw the man's name,

Rose, written in gold letters across a black patch on his chest. "Something big going on in Washington; they got most of the division scrambled."

Weaver spit into a bottle then looked up. "That's bullshit. Something's going down, and once again I'm left out of it. See G-Man, it's shit like this why I never get promoted. I should be in a Crash Hawk ready to drop into the Capital City, not off playing taxi. I'm a combat-hardened killer, not an overpriced escort."

Rose squinted and looked down at him. "You're joking, right? You know what's going on in Washington?"

Weaver shrugged and looked across to Gyles. "What? You mean the fighting?" Gyles said. "The riots? Screw those punks."

The crew chief bit at his lower lip. "You boys really don't know shit, do you?"

"We've been locked down on that damn airfield since they put us on alert," Weaver said. "And Sarge here was jerking off to Sears underwear catalogs, in some mountain cabin up until a few hours ago."

Rose shook his head; his silver eyebrows bunched up, showing worry. He looked down at them sympathetically. "You need to be glad you're not on those Black Hawks. From what the Air Cav people are telling me, Washington is straight hell boiled over. Bad stuff going on in that city."

Gyles looked up at him. "I don't understand. What is it exactly that the local police can't handle?"

"What *isn't* it?" The crew chief shook his head.

"It's like the entire city has gone mad. Let me give you a word of advice, boys. This outbreak, or whatever it is, has people scared, acting in ways that aren't normal. Look, I don't care what they told you or what that kid up there said about this being a simple hop and back," he said, pointing to Howard. "Ignore that; this is real shit you're getting into. I am talking weapons at *condition one*—no bullshit right now. We're going to set you down good and close to the facility. You all need to get in, get your package, and get your ass back to this helicopter, you understand? This rabies shit, or whatever it is, it ain't no joke."

Gyles nodded and watched Rose move away. Then he looked across the aisle to Weaver, who was fighting back a grin. "Guy is a bit of a drama queen, ain't he?" Weaver chuckled.

CHAPTER TWO

Biologic Institute Laboratory Central Virginia

The pair of Chinooks dropped in elevation and cut a wide arc around the city. Looking out the window, Gyles was shocked to see plumes of black smoke rising from the outskirts. Headlights moved on the highway, but what was most prevalent were the strobes of police lights. The helicopter rocked left then moved north. The crew chief looked over the compartment and threw exaggerated motions of waving five fingers to the soldiers.

"Five minutes," Gyles yelled, quickly echoed by the rest of the men as they passed the word. He turned his head and looked out the small port window, seeing what he could have sworn were muzzle flashes. *Fires, police lights, muzzle flashes... what the hell is going on?* He shook his head and pulled at the jacket of the trooper next to him. "Lock and load... pass it down," he shouted. Gyles reached into his own vest, slapped a magazine into the lower receiver of his rifle, and let the bolt go forward. Screw Howard; they wouldn't be going in on empty chambers. He did not have to look up to know that Weaver would be doing the same.

He felt Howard's burning stare and turned his head, making eye contact. The officer showed the palms of his hands. Gyles ignored the expression and shot the doctor a thumbs up. Even though they were issued ammo, Howard was very adamant in explaining this was not a combat operation. In the morning phone call with Michaels, he was told that magazines would stay in their packs; the Fed did not want anyone shooting a toe off, or a negligent discharge destroying property on a civilian interaction. In addition, this was a stateside run, not Iraq. Nobody was going into battle today.

"Somebody's pissed at you, bro," Weaver laughed.

"I can take it." Gyles mockingly made a brushing motion with the glove of his hand across his shoulder. "Let him be butt hurt; something isn't right down there."

Weaver nodded. "Rather be judged by twelve than carried by eight."

"Something like that," Gyles said.

The Chinook increased in speed and banked hard before flaring. When they pulled a tight turn, Gyles felt the Gs in his chest as it spiraled in for a precision landing. *What the hell? Why are they doing a combat landing in a laboratory backyard?* He pulled his neck back and watched the gray sky and distant streetlights transform into the lush tree cover and green grass of a large, well-manicured lawn. The rear ramp of the bird began to lower before the aircraft had even touched the ground. The crew chief was on his feet, holding a strap while speaking loudly to the passengers.

Gyles crunched into his seat as the bird recoiled on its landing gear. Then he quickly snapped to his feet and ushered his men past him, watching them rush into the predawn morning. Gyles waited for Howard, and then joined his side. Together, they exited the aircraft, stepping into the cool Virginia morning air.

"You've got ten mikes, and then we have to be on the outbound leg; we don't have fuel to hang out much longer than that," the chief yelled over the turbines.

Gyles nodded before looking across the landing zone. He could see that the second helicopter had landed over fifty meters to their north. Third and Fourth Squads with Lieutenant Michaels were already fanning out, forming a wide security perimeter that mirrored the one First and Second Squads were building around their own bird. He walked slowly, following Howard into the center of the circle.

Howard looked down at his watch and referred to his notebook. "Well, where are they? It's nearly oh-six. They were supposed to meet us on the east lawn."

Gyles stopped and looked left and right. They were on a long grass field. Behind them to the west were tall, red-brick buildings. Gyles could see the low lights of an empty lobby and, to the front, an empty parking lot. The entire place was cordoned off in tall, black wrought iron fences. In other sections, this fence doubled up with chain link and rolls of concertina wire. Gyles let his eyes wander the perimeter. The security floodlights shone out on empty streets to the south, and, suspiciously, a far-off vehicle gate appeared to be blocked open by an abandoned car.

"Loads of security, but no guards, and the gate's open," he said, waving his hand along the fence line. "Something isn't kosher."

Howard shrugged. "Not business hours, maybe this is normal for them."

"What is this place?" Gyles mumbled.

Howard turned to look at him. "This is where they make vaccines for some of the world's most deadly diseases," he said in a faint voice. The young man twisted, looking in all directions. "I don't understand... the lab people were supposed to be waiting for us with a state police escort. Where is everyone?"

A thundering explosion rumbled in the distance, followed by an orange bloom of light filling the southern sky. Gyles pointed. "Maybe something to do with that? I didn't know the rioting had moved this far from Washington."

The lieutenant shook off the comment. "Ready a squad. If they aren't here, we'll just have to move to them."

"Sir, are you sure about that? If our orders were to rendezvous here, I think we should wait. Count off the ten minutes. If they miss the pickup... so be it."

"Your advice is noted, Sergeant, now ready me a team. I want to check out that building," Howard barked.

Gyles pursed his lips and nodded. "Roger that, sir." He turned away and pointed to Weaver, then spotted motion at the top of the perimeter and stopped.

"Sergeant Gyles! I got somebody in the lobby," a private shouted.

He spun forward, searching the glassed-in entrance of the distant building. He could see a figure in a dark-blue coat pacing the lobby floor. The man was frantic, making jerky motions, his arms flailing wildly. Gyles felt the hairs on the back of his neck begin to stiffen. His senses switched to alert as adrenaline filled his system. He knew something was wrong.

Howard stepped ahead, squinting, his eyes focused on the man in the lobby. "Well, it's about time. I'm going to go have a talk with them and see what's going on. Have the men ready to depart."

Gyles held up an arm, blocking him. "Hold up, Doctor. Something isn't right."

The young man turned back, looking him in the eye, then leaned in close so that the others could not hear. "I'm not sure what's going on with you this morning. I was told you were squared away. First the ammo and now this? Sergeant, you need to get in line with your orders before you are replaced."

The veteran sergeant clenched his jaw and forced a smile before taking a step back. "Yes, sir. But—"

Suddenly, their conversation was broken as the

26

mysterious man shifted position and noticed them. The man stepped forward abruptly and lunged at the lobby doors, its body slamming against them repeatedly. "Sir, that right there isn't normal," Gyles said.

Howard shook his head, edging past the sergeant. Gyles looked to Weaver and waved him forward to join them. Together, they fell in behind the Fed, naturally spacing themselves out to subconsciously guard the man as they approached the lobby. Howard moved quickly up the cement path, only slowing when he heard the muffled echo of screaming snarls from behind the secured shatterproof doors.

As they closed in, Gyles could see that the man was dressed in a state police officer's uniform. His hair and face were coated in dark-red blood, much of it smearing across the glass doors as the man feverishly pounded against them.

"We need a medic up here," Howard shouted over his shoulder. "The infection can't be here, not this fast."

Weaver stepped closer to Gyles. "What kind of mad fuckery is this?" he whispered.

Now fully alert, they moved closer to the man, whose shouts continued to echo through the doors. Howard stopped just short of the handle. He turned back to Gyles, the young man's face now pale white.

"Sergeant?" Howard mumbled. The man's confidence was suddenly lost.

Weaver gasped and stepped back. Gyles turned to him and saw his friend's arm up and pointing. "Ra-

Gyles," he stuttered as his feet pedaled back. The veteran soldier looked up and saw the space Weaver was pointing to. From a darkened hallway, more blood-ied-and-screaming figures were filling the lobby, attracted to the noise of the injured trooper.

"*Sergeant!*" Howard shouted again, his voice now trembling.

Gyles shook off his own fear and pulled his lieu-tenant back, nearly shoving him into Weaver. "Back to the Chinooks; we aren't sticking around to find out what's going on here."

Before an order could be given to fall back, gunfire erupted from the perimeter of the second helicopter—Third and Fourth Platoons were engaged. The trio increased their pace to a running withdrawal with Gyles pulling ahead of the others, rushing to support his men. He could see a mass of bloodied and screaming figures intermixed with the two platoons and Lieutenant Michaels standing in the center of the throng.

"Contact right!" a soldier with Second Squad yelled. Gyles spun to see more figures approaching from the dark to the south. Then a third pack moved out of the shadows, piling over the abandoned car blocking open the vehicle gate. The door gun of the far Chinook roared, opening fire on the mob. Gyles turned to see the frenzied attackers that packed around the fighting men in a bloody flurry now swamped the distant helicopter. "Gyles, they're getting closer," Weaver shouted.

He shook his head, fighting off his own panic and confusion. "What the hell is going on? These aren't protestors, and these aren't rioters," he shouted, looking Howard in the eye. "What do you know about this?"

The lieutenant had locked up, frozen with fear. Gyles reached out and slapped him back to reality. The man stammered and focused on the sergeant's cold stare. "The virus it, it, it—no it can't be here—not yet. Not this fast. This isn't what was forecasted." Howard dropped back, looking in all directions. Seeing they were surrounded, he looked to the waiting helicopter. "They said it wasn't relevant to our mission, it was isolated—that they were just rumors, just *rumors*! It... it can't be here." He took another step closer to the Chinook.

Rose was now hanging off the Chinook's ramp, yelling for them to board. "We have to go! We need to get out of here now!" He looked directly at Gyles with remorse. "Command says the mission is scrubbed, and we don't have the fuel to loiter. We'll have to leave you if you don't get on board."

"Sergeant!" came the panicked scream of a private on the line. Gyles turned back to the horrifying sight of the second Chinook as the pilot attempted to lift off. The helicopter, overwhelmed with the massing mob, listed heavily, its blades digging into the earth. Gyles watched with wide eyes as the chopper crept forward, eating itself then exploding into a ball of fire that ripped through the sky. The heat of the explosion burnt Gyles's face. He turned away, shielding his eyes, only to spot Howard cowering to his front.

Soldiers screamed in confusion all around him. The raging mob was now less than a hundred yards away from their own perimeter. There was no time to break away and board the waiting Chinook; the frenzied civilians would horde and overrun them if they turned their backs to withdraw as Third and Fourth Platoons had done. The helicopter's turbines increased, the rotor wash blowing dust in every direction. He looked again and saw Howard flee into the tail of the helicopter.

Gyles dipped his chin, knowing he had to act. They had to fight or be overrun. He stared at the rifle in his hands. He did not want to kill civilians, but he could not let them take his men. Slowly, he made the sign of the cross then shouted to the soldiers lying on the ground before him. "Open fire on anything moving at us; nothing gets through!" He raised his own weapon and focused on a female in tattered clothing running directly at him. Her eyes and lips black in a disfiguring mask, she showed no signs of stopping. "God forgive us if I'm wrong."

CHAPTER THREE

DAY OF INFECTION PLUS SEVEN, 0630 HOURS

Biologic Institute Laboratory Central Virginia

Gyles dove to the ground, pulling up to his elbows with his rifle tucked into the pocket of his shoulder. The mob was screaming and closing in on them. He could see their bloody, anger-wrenched faces and broken teeth behind torn, blackened lips. Their eyes glowed back at him, dull and lifeless. *What kind of hell have we stepped into?* he thought while letting loose another salvo of rounds, watching the blood-encrusted head of an elderly man snap back with the impact.

"What are these things?" Weaver shouted. "I think we're smack dab in the middle of the Zombie Apocalypse, boys!"

Gyles performed a quick combat reload, locking on to the next runner. "Weaver! Shut up and just kill them!"

A naked man crossed through Gyles's field of vision. The man fell from multiple gunshots, rolled, then pulled back to his feet, running directly at them before the platoon's M240 gunners nearly cut the man in half. More crazed people rushed past the mangled body, running directly into the protective fire created by the heavy machine guns. With both M240s online, they rapid-fired an intersecting pattern, cutting down anything that tried to cross it. He spotted a group running at them from a depression the machine guns couldn't reach. Gyles reached for his hip out of habit, and then clenched his jaw, remembering that they had no grenades ... because *they would not need them* he was told.

"Oh, shit no; we don't need frags, this isn't a combat mission. Well, fuck me running!" He cursed then took a deep breath, watching the enemy numbers in the depression to his front grow.

The rotor blast behind him increased as the Chinook left the ground, the pilots making the tough call to abandon the men and escape the assault. Gyles knew it was the right thing to do, but now they were alone, left to fight their way out. With every round fired, every wave they dropped, he saw the encroaching mass draw closer. The fight was becoming futile. He slid back up to his knees and watched the perimeter collapse around him, like the men at Custer's Last Stand. Second Platoon was drawing in for a final fight. He could see fear and determination on his men's faces; they knew this was the end.

He heard the first of the calls that caused his heart to skip a beat. "Ammo—I'm out!"

Gyles looked, and spun side to side, surveying the perimeter. They had cleared most of them already inside the fences, but the wave of civilians was still pouring over the abandoned car in the open vehicle gate. The outside perimeter fences were holding back the rest. Those trying to climb over were knocked down by the platoon's marksman. At the far sides of the wrought iron, he could see them stacked three deep, fighting to climb over. Anything getting past the gunners now stuck in the fence's concertina wire.

The lobby of the building's glass enclosure was pressed full of bloody faces looking out. Gyles fought the impending doom, his men clearly trapped on all sides... like sitting in the bottom of a mason jar, things pouring over the side and nowhere to run. He shook his head and bit his lip until he tasted blood, watching the madness and knowing there wouldn't be enough ammo to fight their way out. He let the fear and anxiety turn to anger, the way he'd done so many times in the past.

The *pop!* of an M9—his soldiers were down to sidearms. Gyles rose, leaning into the M4, fired another shot, and felt the bolt lock back on an empty chamber. He dropped a hand, searching for his last magazine and sent it home with practiced precision. He took aim on the closest runner, a woman in a yellow sundress, her rage-filled face covered in blood. Before he could press the trigger, the target vanished in a stream of explosive tracers. A blast of mini-gun fire swept the mob and empty parking lot. Swirling lasers etched in from overhead, riddling and tearing bodies apart.

Gyles could hear the cheers of his men. He dropped to his knees then back to his heels and saw the Chinook cutting in from the sky, both left and right door gunners working over the mass, raking the mob with precision. They put a stream of fire into the car at the vehicle gate, causing it to explode, the pyrotechnics hurling a spray of explosive sparks.

The Chinook flared back and gained altitude, making one last high orbit before dropping its nose and making another swooping pass with guns blazing. Gyles spun behind him and saw Weaver getting soldiers on their feet. He was moving them online now, shooting at anything left alive to their front. Gyles hung back, watching as the CH-47 made a wide path around the facility's fences then cut in sharply. It headed directly for the stranded soldiers. Swooping in, it arched up at a steep angle with the ramp open then dropped to the grassy field.

Gyles locked eyes with the crew chief, who was frantically waving at them. "Move!"

The sergeant reached down, lifted the soldier closest to him, and pushed him in the direction of the waiting helicopter. "Fall back, we're leaving," he ordered while reaching down to pull another man to his feet.

He paused to survey the terrain. Looking to the north at the burning hulk of the second CH-47, he saw the bodies of the fallen men from Third and Fourth Squad intermixed with whatever it was that attacked them. Weaver moved up beside him and followed his gaze. "We need to make sure there is no one left alive," Weaver said in a somber tone.

Gyles nodded. "Take a medic and two others." He reached out and grabbed his squad leader's elbow. "Eric, I hate to ask you, but recover their ammo. We're dry here. I don't want to be stuck on the return leg empty-handed."

Weaver dipped his chin. "Roger that; I'll get it done." The man turned, calling for a medic as he directed two others to the north.

A shrill voice from behind said, "Where are they going? We need to get out of here."

Gyles turned his head sharply to see Doctor Howard storming down the ramp of the Chinook at a fast step. He let the doctor draw in close then drew back and threw a stiff, right-hand punch that caught Howard just below the jaw. The doctor reeled back before collapsing to a knee. He stammered and looked up at the platoon sergeant. "I'll have you arrested for that," he gasped.

"I am relieving you; you're not in charge anymore."

"You don't have the authority," Howard said. He pushed back then rolled forward to his hands before attempting to push to his feet.

Gyles stepped in and shouted so everyone could hear. "I am relieving Doctor Howard of any previous authority he commanded due to cowardice. He will be returning with us, but from this point, we will not obey his orders. With the loss of Lieutenant Michaels, I am now in command."

"You think you speak for everyone?" Howard said, pushing out his chest, looking at the men approaching the helicopter.

Soldiers moved past him, scowling, showing their agreement with Gyles. Howard was jostled in the mass of men moving to board the helicopter, the soldiers not taking any caution to avoid him. All of them were clearly aware he'd abandoned them during the attack. Doctor or not, he hadn't stayed to help them.

"You can't do this," Howard said. Staggering back to his feet, he moved to lunge at Gyles.

Before he could, the sergeant closed the distance and raised a fist, causing the doctor to flinch. "You can go quietly, or I can chain you to that vehicle gate and wait for the authorities to collect you."

Howard opened his mouth to continue the argument when Rose appeared, walking down the ramp and holding a length of chain in his hand, which he extended to Gyles. The young doctor eyed the chain cautiously before spinning and moving back onto the Chinook.

Weaver ran up from the shadows, carrying two nylon packs. He stopped at Gyles's side as the rest of his salvage party boarded. "Any survivors?" Gyles asked.

Weaver looked at him, his face a sickly pale. He

slowly shook his head side to side. "Nothing. They were all gone."

Gyles nodded and looked back, making a final check to ensure all his people were aboard. He turned and ushered Weaver ahead of him as they walked up the ramp. As soon as the helicopter was airborne with the ramp up, Weaver moved to the jump seat next to Gyles and pressed his face close. "Something ain't right. The bodies... those things... I'm not sure they were human."

"What do you mean?"

"I don't know... but our guys? They were more than dead." Weaver looked down, his expression sour. He put a hand to his face and wiped away beads of sweat. "They"—he paused, taking in a shallow breath —"They were torn apart, and some looked like they'd been chewed on. And... the other things? The way they looked, the injuries... the wounds... they should have been dead themselves. Those weren't people."

Gyles grimaced, searching for a response, when Howard pushed his way to the back of the helicopter. He stood over the sergeant and yelled, "Command will hear about this when we get back to Stewart."

The crew chief, still standing at the back ramp, moved close and shook his head. "Not going back to Stewart."

"What?" Gyles asked, ignoring Howard.

"Not enough fuel. We burned too much making the gun run and coming back for you."

"Well, we do appreciate that, Rose."

"Wasn't a totally selfless act," Rose said. "When they found out we hadn't recovered the medical team, command wouldn't transmit the next waypoint, and then Hunter Field waved us off—wouldn't let us return home. They're under attack, and they've lost the airfield. Bastards turned us around and said locate an alternate spot."

"Lost the airfield? Alternate?"

"Yeah, that's what they said. Without the medical team, we aren't worth the risk of a quick reaction force. They don't need us anymore... no alternate pickup, no orders."

Gyles looked back at his tired men in the compartment behind him. "What the hell do they expect us to do?"

"I don't know. We were trying to figure that out when we lost radio contact."

"Wait, lost contact? How is that possible?"

Rose put a thumb over his shoulder, pointing to a port window. "I think you know how it's possible. All the channels are broadcast storms. Everyone out there is screaming for help on every open channel; nearly impossible to get a message through. Whatever fight we're in, we're losing it."

Gyles stared blankly, attempting to process all the information. "Stewart is really gone? Hunter is gone?"

Rose shrugged his shoulders. "No, not gone; they're fighting, just too busy for us. Pilots are trying to figure out right now where to park us."

Gyles nodded and went to stand, looking toward the cockpit.

"Wait—where are you going? We aren't finished here," Howard said, reaching out for him. Gyles quickly moved out of the way. Catching the doctor's wrist, he bent it upward and maneuvered the man down and into the jump seat next to Weaver.

"Keep an eye on this deserter. If he can't control himself, chain him up." He then turned and looked at Rose.

"Could you take me to the pilots?"

CHAPTER FOUR

DAY OF INFECTION PLUS SEVEN, 0710 HOURS.

Over Central Virginia

He held the headset close, blocking out the sounds of the aircraft noise, his mind filled with overlapping broadcasts. Men in combat, panicked units overrun. Commands trying to get messages through, stepped on by other units begging for help. Fighter aircraft dropping ordnance on strategic bridges, trying to slow the advance, struggling to communicate with men in the fight. This was Iraq and Afghanistan, not the southern United States. He paused and shook his head; he hadn't even experienced this much terror overseas. This was new, and he had no idea what to do.

Gyles held his hand to the earpiece while looking at Rose. "Where is this at?"

"Where? This is everywhere. Most of it is just outside Washington D.C., but we also have contacts in Atlanta, Nashville, Birmingham, as far south as

Tampa, and every population center and highway in between."

"I don't understand how this is spreading so fast... What the hell are we dealing with?"

The co-pilot, the back of his helmet stenciled with the name *Mitchell* in black lettering, looked over his shoulder, making eye contact. "We've all been lied to. This isn't some bullshit uprising. That shit we saw out there was something else. The flight crews dropping troops off at the Capital warned us about it. Called them zombies and monsters. Heck, who can blame us for not believing them?" Mitchell said. "Listen, Sergeant, I don't know what you have going on with that kid back there, but he knows more than he's letting on. Get it sorted out. We won't have time to play games once we're back on the ground."

Gyles frowned and looked forward through the windscreen as dawn revealed black pillars of smoke in all directions. On the ground, he could see burning homes, flashing lights from emergency vehicles, and convoys of civilian caravans crowding and congesting the highways.

"Where are we going?" He could see they were traveling north with the rising sun to their right.

Mitchell turned, glancing at the pilot. "We tried for Richmond's main airport, but those things are all over the ground. The LZ is too hot." Mitchell pointed to a small paper map folded square and pinned in a laminated case. "I know a spot; it's an Army National Guard post—it's not much, but I grew up near there as a kid. They call it the Vineyard—far west of here, and better yet, it backs up to the George Washington and Jefferson National Forests, so it's far enough away from population centers. It'll take us away from the fighting and give us a chance to catch our breath and refit until it's clear to return to Stewart."

"You've been able to reach them? You've got radio comms?" Gyles asked, staring at the small black square on the map surrounded by green terrain indicators.

"Had a brief conversation with their commanding officer before we were cut off."

Gyles was silent for a moment before lifting his chin at the map. "So– this National Guard post...?"

"It's a small joint, not much more than an emergency field, but a good enough place to lick our wounds and regroup. They haven't seen any of the things in their area, but—"

"But what?" Gyles asked, leaning in.

Mitchell moved his hand to the radio console and expertly dialed in a frequency. Gyles's headset boomed with chatter and beeps. More cries for help, but different from before; these were civilians—911 dispatchers, police officers, first responders.

"What is this?" Gyles asked, his eyes closed and hand pressing the earpiece tight to his head, trying to isolate the voices.

"State police. It's their closed network. I've tried pinpointing some of the calls," he said, looking at the map. "I don't think there's a single region in the state that is untouched. You need to expect to find them on the ground when we touch down."

"What the hell is going on?"

"I don't know; the one you need to be asking is cowering back there." Mitchell pointed a thumb behind him.

The sergeant dipped his chin in agreement, waiting for Mitchell to dial back the radio. "National Guard armory then? What kind of unit are they?"

"Aviation, Black Hawks mostly, but don't get excited; all of their assets have been deployed to Andrews Air Force Base near D.C. All they got on site are some staff and admin left behind."

"How long until we land?" Gyles asked.

"Less than ten mikes. We'll make another wide orbit then bring us in. Have your men ready to go. They'll be looking to you to provide security down there."

Gyles nodded. Still thinking about the soldiers he left on the field, he turned and looked at the worried faces of his men. "We can do that."

Mitchell reached out a hand to slap his arm. "Don't get too comfortable down there. As soon as we gas this hooker up and get clearance from Stewart, we're hitting the trail again."

CHAPTER FIVE

DAY OF INFECTION PLUS SEVEN, 0750 HOURS.

Over Central Virginia.

"Let's have a chat with Doctor Howard."

The crew chief smirked and turned back to the rear troop hold, leading the way to the now bound and gagged medical man. Two beefy corporals flanked the doctor on each side, holding him in place. His hands were in his lap, thick black zip ties fastening them together.

Weaver smirked and looked at Gyles. "I would have put a sandbag over his head, too, if I'd had one."

"Did I miss something?" Gyles asked, positioning himself so that he faced the doctor. "What's with the restraints?"

Weaver pointed at the bound man's chest. "He wouldn't shut up about you—and how he's going to have you locked up. He tried to get to his weapon. Said he would have you executed when we get back to Stewart."

Before Gyles could comment, Howard attempted to lunge out of his seat. The corporals quickly snatched him and slammed him back into the webbing. Gyles shook his head and pointed an index finger at the gag. "Take it off."

Howard lunged as the gag was removed from his mouth, the soldiers pulling him back into the seat yet again. "Kill the theatrics," Gyles barked in response. "I need to know what the hell is going on out there."

"What are you talking about?" Howard shouted.

"The mission, the medical team... all of it. What the hell happened?"

Rose put a hand to his headset and looked at Gyles. "On the ground in five."

Howard overheard the comment and smiled. "This will all be over for you soon. I'll have you arrested as soon as we land."

Letting loose his rage, Gyles didn't hold back. He threw a quick jab, snapping the man's head against the fuselage. When the doctor leaned forward, his lips were cut where they'd impacted with freshly broken teeth. The veins in Gyles's neck bulged. "You want to make threats? Well, in that case, let's make this interesting." Gyles let loose another quick punch when he saw that no one would intervene on the doctor's behalf. "I left most of my platoon dead on the field back there. Men that were my friends. I know their families. Men that I was responsible for. Do you think I care what happens to me now? Do you really want to test me?

"Hell, arrest me. I just want to know why they died!" he shouted, throwing another jab.

This time Rose stepped in and pulled Gyles back. "Okay, he's had enough. I'm sure the kid is ready to talk to you."

Howard's head slumped forward and slowly came up, blood pouring from both of his nostrils. With a broken nose and swollen lips, the young man's arrogance was gone. He looked at Gyles and said, "You already know it all; we went to get a medical team. Vaccine specialists. It's not like I wrote the damn orders. It was your job. You idiots can't blame me for this."

"I want to know the rest. That wasn't a riot we saw down there, those were not protestors," the sergeant said through gritted teeth, flexing his gloved hand while looking at the bloodied spots on his knuckles.

"There is no 'rest'! What you saw is what I know."

Gyles snarled and feigned another jab then, instead, reached for his sidearm and chambered a round before sticking it under Howard's jaw. The doctor tried to pull away.

Rose put up his hands, looking Gyles in the eye. "Easy son. Easy."

"Fuck that! He talks or he loses the top of his head." Gyles scowled.

"Okay, okay. There is an outbreak. We don't know what it is or how to control it. It's not rioting, it's not the damn flu... it's something else. Something new... something worse."

"What is it?" Gyles said, now pressing his face close and yelling at the officer. "Talk to me or stop talking forever."

Howard shook his head. "It's classified; I can't."

This time Gyles did not feign, delivering a stiff blow to the man's midsection, causing him to bend over and gasp for air. "I'm running out of patience, and we are both almost out of time."

"Goddammit, stop!" Howard yelped. "They call it *Primalis Rabia*."

"What do you mean *Primal what*?"

Howard looked down at his bound hands. "It's a bio attack, an engineered weapon. It was triggered across the globe all at once."

"Attacked by who?" Gyles asked. "Russians? China?"

Howard shook his head. "Not the Russians or China; so far, they've been hit the hardest."

"Who then?"

Exhaling through pursed lips, Howard reeled back. "The sons of Bin Laden. They are a group operating out of—"

"I know who they are," Gyles said. "They hit the embassy last month, killed the ambassador, and overran it. No survivors."

Howard nodded. "There was more to it than that. The Marine commander on the ground confirmed he was fighting the infected. He is the one that called in the bone strike on his own position that ended the attack. Autopsies confirmed the infection."

"Bone?" Gyles asked.

Rose leaned in. "B-One, Bone."

Shaking his head, the platoon sergeant looked at Howard with suspicion. "That was a month ago. If we knew about it then, why wasn't the alert sent out?"

"It had to stay secret. Governments were warned, but they all reacted differently to the intelligence—most with disbelief. We couldn't just sound a general alarm. We didn't want the sons jumping the gun before we were ready."

"A lot of good that did," Rose said. "You said these attacks were everywhere and simultaneously?"

Howard swallowed. "Yes...Europe, Africa, Asia... they left no stone unturned. We had some warning they were coming, and we tried to stop it here. We shut down the borders. But it moves too quickly, hours from contact to infection and... well, it's what we saw out there this morning."

Weaver moved in close, interjecting. "Your story is bullshit, Doc. Hit him again, Sarge."

"No, no, no, it's true. Colonel Cloud knows all about it; he wrote these orders. He was the one that sent the team in to investigate the lab in Virginia. They said they were close to a vaccine."

Gyles put up a hand and moved Weaver back. "You said there was an attack? How come we haven't heard about this? There has been no news about a bio-attack."

"I told you. It was worldwide; they triggered it globally through the airports. Martyrs armed with needles infected themselves in populated areas... Focus hasn't been on the incidents because we have been entirely consumed on stopping the spread."

Weaver shook his head and prepared to speak, Gyles again raising a hand to silence him. "You said we had advanced warning that this was coming?"

"Some. Somehow our intelligence guys discovered the plan. Rumor was one of the intended martyrs turned himself in to authorities. We tried to stop it, but obviously failed." Howard shook his head. "I'm telling you the truth."

Gyles brought his hand up to rub his chin, then nodded for the doctor to continue.

"I don't know all of the details, but the mission failed. The Whitehouse ordered the borders sealed, grounded all air traffic last weekend. We watched it spread around the world and thought we'd stopped it at the border wall. But then a day or two ago, it began popping up here."

"Then?" Gyles asked, already knowing the answer. "Why not report it for what it was? Why are we calling it riots when you know what it really is?"

"That's all above my paygrade." Howard dropped his head, then lifted it again to lock eyes with the platoon sergeant. "Giving too much alarm would have caused panic. People would have fled, and we would have lost control of it. We needed people to lock up and shelter in place. Colonel Cloud thought it could be contained if we moved fast enough, that it would burn itself out. We thought the infected would wither and die, but they don't; they get stronger. The CDC thought if we could hold it back until a vaccine or a cure could be developed, we'd be okay. That's why we were tasked to get the researchers."

The gear flexed beneath the Chinook as it touched down. Rose, having heard enough, finally interrupted. "Well, we know it's out now, and we failed to get those vaccine docs. Stewart is on lockdown, and we're homeless. Is there anything else you can tell us before I drop this ramp?"

With his eyes closed, Howard muttered, "If it's out there, there isn't anything we can do. We're all dead."

Gyles looked back at Rose. "I think we're done here." Rose nodded and worked the controls, dropping the ramp.

"What about him, Sergeant?" Weaver asked, looking down at the medical doctor.

"Keep him locked up until I can figure out what to do with him."

CHAPTER SIX

The Vineyards National Guard Armory Vines, Virginia.

With Howard's rants of innocence still filling the air behind him, Gyles made his way down the ramp and onto the cold asphalt tarmac. The temperatures were lower here, and a heavy blanket of fog covered the surrounding terrain. Spinning in a three-sixty, he could see empty pads where rotary aircraft had been, refueling carts, and a row of parked vehicles neatly aligned along a distant hangar.

Directly to his front sat a tall, olive-drab, steel building. A cartoon image of a bald eagle with blood-covered talons squeezing a lifeless crow was painted on a large overhead door, 147th Aviation stenciled in dark-blue lettering below it. A tall fence topped with concertina wire ringed the entire compound. A long sliding gate was chained shut, and on the far side was a blacktop parking lot filled with civilian vehicles. Shifting his eyes, he could not spot any guards or ground crews.

Gyles stepped closer to the fence and saw they were situated on a hilltop overlooking a small town. In the early morning light, he could still see the glow of streetlights and the sparkle of homes. A loud *screech* and *clunk* turned his attention back to the steel building. He watched a tall, lanky man approach him from a heavy steel door. The man was dressed in a dark-green flight suit, with a black badge identifying him as *Col A. Jessup*. Alongside the officer walked two younger soldiers in Army Combat Uniform (ACU) fatigues, carrying M4 rifles.

"Colonel." Gyles saluted as the man closed the distance.

The colonel returned his salute and fixed his eyes at the rear of the Chinook. "This all you brought?"

The sergeant looked back at his men pouring down the ramp. Weaver was already busy breaking them into teams and positioning the soldiers along the security fence. "Yes, sir. We lost our second bird and half the platoon, including my LT."

The older man grimaced then nodded. "I got the word from your air crew." Jessup watched the men running to the perimeter. "We're all in a world of hurt, I'm afraid."

"Any word from the outside?" Gyles asked.

The colonel looked at him hard. "I sent my squadron to Andrews Airforce Base this morning to provide air cover and support to the Capital Police Department. Last word I had, the base was overrun. All my people pulled back and moved farther south. Fort Belvoir is the new staging area. I got nothing else in the last two hours; we're in the dark. The only damn news I'm getting now is on the TV, and they are censoring the hell out it. I was hoping you could *tell* me something!"

"Sir?" Gyles looked at him blankly.

"What in the fuck is going on?" Jessup asked. "I get woke up at midnight, ordered to recall my squadron, ordered to send every swinging dick I got into the Capital to provide air support. Now they are all off the net, and I got no comms with them. The news shows Washington and Atlanta on fire. No offense to you and your men, but out of the blue I get a shot-up and thirsty bird full of air assault grunts requesting to land in my backyard and borrow some of my gas."

"Colonel, we weren't shot up. It's worse than that."

Jessup tightened his brow. "You said you lost half your platoon. I assumed it was from the riots coming out of Washington."

"No." Gyles dipped his chin and looked back at the bound medical man still sitting in the Chinook's jump seat. Rose and other members of the flight crew were scrambling around the Chinook, already beginning the refueling procedures. "Something far worse is happening—" Before he could finish, a single gunshot followed by a loud scream echoed in from the small town below them.

The sergeant spun on his heels, instinctively bringing up his rifle. He could see Sergeant Weaver was already kneeling at the gate beside another soldier, a set of scout binoculars in his hands. "You see anything, Weaver?" Gyles called out.

"Nothing," the squad leader answered without looking back. More gunfire echoed, chaotic screams filling the still air.

Gyles stepped closer and put a gloved hand on the chain link of the fence, pulling against it as if he was testing its strength, the colonel shadowing him as they stood looking through the gate. On the far side, the drive veered off into the civilian visitors' lot and then wound down the hill, passing through light tree cover before finally meeting a line of large brick buildings reminiscent of any small town's main street. Beyond that were smaller homes and neighborhoods. Gyles's head shifted left and right along the front perimeter with his rifle still at the low ready.

"This isn't a strategic position, if that's what you're thinking; just an armory," Jessup said, moving closer. "If the violence moves here, we'll be in trouble. I don't see it holding."

More salvos of gunfire echoed. A distant police siren joined the chaotic symphony of sounds as the screams intensified.

Gyles made a quick turn, surveying the grounds, then looked back at the colonel. "We've got the high ground; we can make this work for a while. All we need to do is gas up the bird, and we can be on our way.

How many people do you have here? I'm sure we can squeeze you all in."

Jessup pulled back against the fence and leaned in closer. "Sergeant, you still haven't said what it is we're up against."

The veteran soldier turned and faced him. "You ever watched one of those movies where everyone has gone mad? Monsters come out of the dark for no reason to attack and kill everything they can get at? Well, it's like that, only a million times worse. They surrounded and overran us in a matter of minutes. They ran full-sprint into my shooters. They took out two of my squads, swarming and tearing my men apart with their bare hands. Colonel, these were not rioters or panicked civilians fleeing an outbreak. Whatever it was, they came at us and showed no mercy, no restraint. They didn't stop until we killed every one of them."

When Gyles paused and met the colonel's eyes, the older man's face had turned pale. "Then the stories are true?"

"Stories?"

"We had reports come in from the air crews. Unbelievable things about police roadblocks destroyed. Hospitals attacked with no survivors; nurses, doctors, the wounded... everyone dead. We–we thought it was just the fog of war; you know, panicked soldiers talking shit."

From the city, more sirens filled the air as a stream of automatic weapons fire was followed by an explosion that flashed a glow of light and a bright ball of fire into the sky. Jessup looked in the direction of the flames and pointed. "That's Vines's only fuel station. What the hell is happening down there?"

Gyles bit his lower lip. "Get your people rounded up and ready to move. We can't stay here long. We'll have to find another spot or see if we can get to Fort Belvoir... convoy out over road if we have to."

The colonel spun around and grabbed Gyles's shoulder. He shook his head solemnly. "Sergeant, we can't leave. And this place won't hold up without your help." Jessup looked toward the steel-walled building then pointed at the nearly full visitor parking lot outside the fence. "I have civilians inside. Some of the soldiers brought their families to camp for safekeeping before they rolled out this morning. How was I supposed to turn them away?"

"You have family members inside the armory?" Gyles furled his brow. "Are you serious? In there?"

Jessup frowned and shook his head. "I had to allow it. What choice did I have? Half my people wouldn't have shown up for duty if I refused. Presidential order and backing of the governor or not, these are National Guard troops. Our families don't have a base to go to like your active duty guys. You do *not* just wake them up in the middle of the night and say come to work. Your families are in danger but leave them and get here. Especially with Washington all over the news and broadcasters talking about civil war. My people are dedicated, but they wouldn't abandon their families."

Jessup paused before saying, "I wouldn't have asked them to."

Gyles nodded his understanding. "Okay, they are here, so now what?"

"I don't know... Hell, I had no idea things would be this bad when my boys departed this morning."

"Well, you aren't alone on that assumption," Gyles grunted. "How many are in there? What kind of numbers are we talking about?"

Jessup put his hand to his chin and dragged his fingers over the gray stubble. "Over a hundred. I had a few more come through the gate a couple hours ago. Some of my troops were able to get a call home before they moved again to Fort Belvoir. With what they saw in Washington, they sent their families to the armory. I know it violates protocol, but like I said, we won't turn away our own."

Gyles looked back at his men behind him. He wiped sweat from his forehead before saying, "My people have families too. I'd want Stewart to take them in if they could."

"We all have someone," Jessup said.

"Your family here?" Gyles asked.

Jessup frowned and sighed. "No—they are with my wife out West, touring college campuses. I was supposed to travel out and meet them this weekend." The colonel rubbed his eyes. "What about you, Sergeant? You have family out there?"

Gyles shrugged. "She's with her parents up North."

"I'm sure she'll be fine."

Gyles nodded his head, exhaling loudly, then turned to look back at Weaver. The soldier shot him a shrug and grinned. Gyles knew his people would stick with him no matter what he decided. If they got back on the Chinook and left now, nobody would question him. They wouldn't leave these people defenseless after what they'd just seen. Gyles turned back to the colonel and said, "We got your back, sir. We ain't going nowhere; not without everyone."

CHAPTER SEVEN

The Vineyards National Guard Armory Vines, Virginia.

"You know if they come the way they did at the lab, we won't be able to stop them, G-Man," Weaver said as he walked the armory with Gyles, inspecting the preparations. "What the hell are we doing here?"

The remaining men of India Company, Second Platoon, were working feverishly to reinforce the compound. The soldiers had seen the enemy firsthand, and that fear motivated them to get things right. The armory's vehicles were now parked defensively in every corner, the open hatches of the armored Humvees ready with the platoon's own machine gunners mounting their weapons in the turrets.

The soldiers moved methodically, the way they'd done just a few months ago in the desert. It wasn't a new practice for his men to move in and secure a compound. It was old hat for them, but this flavor of fear was new, and it was a new kind of enemy. They were on edge and jumpy; they wanted to be far away from all of it. The men wanted to go home, they wanted to hear from their families, they wanted to mourn for their friends. Even in the war zone, they hadn't faced the losses like they had that morning.

Gyles watched his men prep the armored vehicles, each now topped off with fuel. The platoon sergeant hoped the men could drop into the armored vehicles and use them for cover if the things breached the outer walls. The Chinook remained in the same spot. Fully fueled, it was ready to launch and provide air support until its guns ran dry.

Rose and the men of the air crew stoically guarded the rear ramp, ready to go at a moment's notice. The pilots had suggested using the bird to ferry the civilians to Fort Belvoir. If they packed it full, they could do it in three to four round trips. After considering it would take most of the day, and that the noise of the Chinook would bring attention to the camp, they dismissed the idea. There was also a real concern that once the CH-47 arrived at Belvoir, they would not be allowed to leave again, effectively stranding all of them without air support.

The sergeant swallowed dryly and watched men pull a long string of wire outside the perimeter. The armory had shipping containers full of gear, and his men were having a good time utilizing it. It was easier to reinforce this existing position than to start over somewhere else. Desperate for every hour, every hour was used to build up the compound. He waited nervously, the intensity of the violence in the distant town increasing. He knew it was only a matter of time before it reached them up on the hilltop.

Weaver stepped closer and looked at his friend. "You okay, man? You hear me?"

Gyles nodded.

"What are we doing here?" he said, repeating the question.

Gyles walked to the fence and turned around. "Hell, I don't know... is there any place else to go?" he whispered. "I don't think there is. We've got to hold."

Automatic weapons fire rattled through the valley below them, the rhythmic reports coming in on the wind. Police sirens sang a steady hymn, letting the soldiers know that the blue line was still holding. For how long? That was another question.

"We should mount up and roll out of here while we can," Weaver said. "We have enough wheels to roll everyone back to Stewart."

Gyles nodded. "I don't know." He had thought of the same thing himself. "That's a long trip with a lot of people we don't know."

"Well, if we stay, we need to know what's going on down there," Weaver said. "If the locals are fighting, we should lean into that. Might be something we can do to help, or at least keep the fight tied up and away from the armory."

Gyles was no stranger to war. He knew Weaver was right; the best way to prevent attacks against a patrol base was to patrol. Right now, this was his base, and it was full of civilians who he'd been charged to keep alive. He needed to treat it that way and stop thinking of it as a hiding place. The only way he knew to do that properly was to close in and destroy the enemy. It didn't matter what this enemy was. He would push his doctrine and training to the max to protect these people. If he failed, at least it would be standing his ground and not huddling in the corner of some basement.

"I know," Gyles answered. He thought about the civilians inside and wondered about the families of his own men. "You still have that red-haired girl back in Clarksville?" he said, trying to change the subject.

Weaver smiled and looked away. "Nah, she forgot to tell me about her husband. Guess he got paroled while we were in the sandbox. He was pissed off to find my shit hanging in the bedroom closet."

Gyles laughed and turned to slap Weaver on the back. "Sorry about that, bro. What did I tell you about hunting for wives in those trailer parks?"

"Whatever, man, that chick was hot. And she made a mean meatloaf too. Hey, did you manage to work things out with Tracy?"

Gyles sighed and shook his head. "Nope, she packed up and moved in with her folks. I found divorce papers on the kitchen table at the apartment, everything moved out. Once I thought we could patch things up, but not anymore. She won't even return my calls."

"She must have a man on the side then."

"Wow, thanks for the confidence boost, brother," Gyles said, shaking his head.

"Hey, who knows... after all this, maybe you'll get that shot at a second chance."

"I don't know; she never was cut out for the army life. Her dad told me to move on when I called him at his office." He looked down at his boots then out toward the distant town. "Maybe I should call her now. I bet they have no idea what's going on."

"Colonel says the phones are down," Weaver said. "Cell circuits are hosed." The squad leader frowned and dug through a pocket on his sleeve. He slapped a small tin of smokeless tobacco against his palm and offered some to his friend. "Forget about it. It was fun while it lasted, right? Guess guys like us are just meant to stay single."

"You get a feel on the rest of the men?" Gyles asked.

"Like us, they just want to get home. Not knowing what's going on is bothering the guys."

Gyles nodded; that was enough for now, but soon it wouldn't be.

"What about the town? You thinking recon?" Weaver asked, quickly getting back on subject.

Gyles turned and waved off the tobacco, a smile breaking his lips. "Recon? More like cannonball run."

"Love that movie," Weaver grunted. "What do you got in mind?"

Gyles rolled his neck, a loud pop reverberating from his shoulders. He shrugged, adjusting the heavy body armor. "We're nearly out of food for the M4s, and even with what you recovered from the casualties, we'll be down to stick fighting if they come at us in the numbers we saw this morning. The colonel said they don't have much either; a few cans of 5.56 for the members of his guard force. Most of the ammo they drew went downrange with his battalion. The rest of their ordnance is stored hours from here, in a bunker. Might as well be on the moon with those things out there."

"Not exactly giving a pep talk right now, are you, G-man?"

"I'm still trying to wrap my head around this. This kind of thing isn't in the book." He nodded. "You hear that gunfire down there? Those are carbines. The police are expending a lot of 5.56, probably military surpluses, but more than likely shit better than ours. I say we load up two trucks and visit the local cop shop."

"Why not just dial 9-1-1 and ask them if they have any extra?"

"Yeah, smartass, because nobody has thought of doing that yet, did they? Like you said, phone lines are all down; Jessup tried earlier. They're just drawing a busy signal on the landlines, and the radios are buzzed full of traffic. He says the department has their own radio net, but they haven't had any luck connecting to it."

Weaver grimaced and furrowed his brow. "So, say we get down there, then what? Not like they're just going to give us their ammo cache."

"Colonel says it's a small department—less than five fulltime officers, and another half dozen part-time volunteers and part-time deputies. Maybe we can offer our help in exchange for a resupply."

Weaver chuckled. "Or we roll up like we own the place, take over the mission and everything that goes along with it."

"Yeah, cause a second battle we can't win is just what we need right now," Gyles said. "Just get a pair of trucks ready. We'll take First Squad for a walk and see what's going on out there." The platoon sergeant squinted, not taking his eyes off the distant town. "Bring Howard too; we'll need a doctor if the infected really are here."

Weaver nodded, stuffing a large wad of tobacco into his cheek. "And where will you be?"

Gyles motioned toward the steel building with his head. "I need to check out the rest of this place and talk to the old man. Be ready to move when I get back." He turned toward the building and the civilians he knew were inside, the ones he'd been avoiding since his arrival at the armory.

In front of the building, near the pedestrian door, the two guards he had seen earlier were standing watch. One with his rifle slung, the other with it leaning against the wall. Neither of the men bothered to acknowledge him as he approached. Gyles changed his course and stopped just inches from the senior of the two soldiers. A fat-faced corporal, he had his rifle carelessly slung over a shoulder with a cigarette dangling from his lips. Gyles knew from experience that complacency and lack of discipline could destroy morale faster than any enemy.

"So what exactly is it you're supposed to be doing here, Corporal?" Gyles asked in a sharp tone.

The soldier slowly looked up at Gyles, still showing little recognition of his authority. "Colonel wants us to guard the door," he said smugly.

"Is that a two-man job?" Gyles retorted.

"Colonel sai—"

"You don't trust my soldiers to cover the door?" Gyles interrupted, not allowing the corporal to finish. "Why the hell are you smoking and joking while the rest of this camp busts its ass to reinforce it?" Gyles shouted. "Don't you care what happens here?"

The soldiers suddenly realized they were in trouble and both snapped to attention, the cigarette falling from the man's lip to the ground. "Sergeant, we were told to watch the door, just following—"

"Where are you from, Corporal?" Gyles asked, stepping closer, his face now only inches from the man.

"Vines, Sergeant," the corporal said.

"You're *from* here?" Gyles was tired; his body hurt and he was still holding back the resentment about being kept in the dark about the real situation he had blindly led his men into. He knew better than to take it out on these men, but he was running on the edge. He took a step back and looked at the man's nametape on his chest. "Jones, is it?" he asked, not wanting an answer. "Jones, grab your shit; you're going to be taking a trip with me into town. I need someone local to show me around."

"But, Sarnt, Vines isn't safe; there's been shooting coming from there."

Gyles grabbed the man by the collar and pulled him in. "Didn't you just say you were from Vines?"

"Ya, yes, Sar–Sergeant," he said, stuttering.

"And you don't give a shit about what's going on down there?" Gyles asked him coldly.

The man's jaw dropped but he didn't answer; instead, he stared at Gyles with his mouth hanging open.

Gyles nodded. "Get your shit and find Sergeant Weaver. We leave in ten." He pushed the corporal aside and pulled open the door.

Entering the building, he knew what he was walking into, but the sight of it still shocked him. The door led into a large open drill deck the size of a double basketball court. Every bit of flooring was filled with civilians and their bags, along with foldable army cots lined up in rows. Soldiers walked among the families, handing out bottles of water and brown, plastic MRE packages. At the end of the room, people waited in line for a single restroom; the building was obviously not equipped for the current number of occupants.

At the far end of the room was an open classroom area with tables and chairs situated around a pair of plasma televisions currently tuned into national network news. Amidst the crowd of people gathered there, Gyles recognized Jessup, with the pilots of the Chinook standing next to him. As Gyles made his way across the congested space, women and children looked up at him with weary faces. He tried to force a reassuring smile or a nod of his head as he passed them.

He could tell by their eyes and expressions that they were fully aware of the situation closing in all around them. On the TV, a reporter spat rapid-fire updates, subtitles painted along with her words while the scrolling bar at the bottom listed names of major cities now under martial law. The world was burning, and he was caught up on the frontlines of it all.

Jessup noticed him and pulled away from the crowd. Walking toward a narrow hallway with the pilots in tow, he signaled for Gyles to follow. They passed to the end of the hallway then stepped into a small conference room. The white walls of the room were covered with motivational posters and wall charts of the local geography. One long wall contained a large, plate-glass window covered with partially drawn blinds. Through the window, Gyles could see a large, cut lawn that overlooked the town. High in a corner of the room was another flat-panel television showing the same broadcaster's face.

Jessup moved to the end of the table and dropped heavily into a leather chair. His left hand stroked the top of his head before he locked his tired eyes on Gyles. "I understand you're holding your commander on board the Chinook."

"No, sir; Lieutenant Michaels died fighting. He was KIA with Third and Fourth Squads. The man I'm holding is Doctor Howard. He's a medical officer with the Centers for Disease Control. And yes, he is still aboard the Chinook. Just trying to keep him safe, sir; he has a habit of running off."

Jessup rubbed his hands together and looked to Mitchell, the CH-47 copilot. "Yes, I heard. You can turn him over to me now. We can take care of him here."

"Thank you for the offer, sir, but we'll keep him with us for now. He's the only one that seems to have any idea what the hell is going on." Gyles grinned, hoping the colonel would take it for what it was and not push the issue. "Which is why I came to see you. I was hoping you had current information for me. Any word from the higher-ups?" Gyles asked.

Jessup slowly shook his head. "I'm afraid not. I tried to reach your command at Stewart; everything is down or tied up with priority traffic. Cell circuits are dead and the landlines are all blocked."

"Nothing at all then?"

Jessup put a hand on the table and lifted a sheet of paper. "We've gotten an emergency order over the secure fax. It came in somehow, but we haven't been able to send a response or reach anyone for follow-up. I have a man retrying every five minutes."

"No Internet?" Gyles asked.

"The entire network is down. Can't handle the surge of people trying to check in. This is an armory; if we were on a base we would be plugged into the defense networks, but out here we are on civilian lines. We rely on local services, and I have no way to hit the secure networks."

"What were the orders, the fax?"

Jessup slid the paper across the table. Below the address and header information was a set of typed instructions. Gyles read them aloud. "All units in the field are instructed to hold position. Secure your location and civilian populations when possible. Hold position. Do not combine units or populations. Do not attempt transit without explicit instruction." He pushed the paper back. "That's it?"

"I think the worm has turned—we're headed in a different direction."

Gyles's eyes went wide. "Turned?"

"We've lost any momentum. They're shifting us into a defensive posture. I suspect the next move will be setting up roadblocks and checkpoints. Maybe even taking out bridges and highways. Creating new choke-points to slow the spread."

"How...? Why do you think that?"

"That line about holding position and not combing populations... They are trying to stop the spread." Jessup lifted a coffee cup and considered the stained empty mug. He set it back down and sighed. "It's a logical move. They failed to lock it all down and quarantine the red zones early on. Slowing the spread is all that's left. If I was a betting man, I'd guess bombing will be next. They want us dug in and holding while the Air Force hits anything on the move. They'll start getting aggressive against high populations of the infected."

Gyles looked down at the table. "How long until that happens? I've seen these things; it might slow them down, but if they hit the cities it's just going to push more of them right to us."

Jessup spun in the chair and looked up at the television. A reporter stood on a hilltop. In the distance, blooms of black smoke roiled on the horizon. Footage flashed of highways congested with traffic, hospital emergency rooms filled with screaming people. "It's already started. Sergeant, what can we do to keep this place safe until someone can come to reinforce us?"

The sergeant bit his lower lip and pushed away from the table. "Sir, I'm taking two trucks into town. We're red on ammo, and if we don't find some, we won't be able to stop anything that comes for us." Gyles looked up and pointed at the window and shook his head. "This place needs to be locked down and barricaded."

"What do you suggest?"

"These windows are no good. You need to cover every entrance and every opening that leads outside the perimeter. Be ready to barricade that hallway that leads back into the drill deck. We may lose this front office area if they come at us in large numbers. Move the guards you have on the door and get them up on the roof as lookouts."

Jessup looked to a young officer on his right. The man nodded and took notes. "We can do that," Jessup said.

CHAPTER EIGHT

The Vineyards National Guard Armory Vines, Virginia.

Two up-armored vehicles roared through the open gates of the armory, a gunner in each turret, the other passengers with windows open and weapons out at the ready. The platoon sergeant rode shotgun in the lead Humvee, while Weaver commanded the vehicle behind them. Gyles looked left at his driver, the young, freckled, Corporal Jones in clean Army Combat Uniform, his rifle pinned to a clip near the driver's door. In the back seat behind the driver, Howard rode with his back stiff and rigid.

"We going to have a problem, Doc?" Gyles asked, speaking loudly over the vehicle's engine.

Howard mumbled something under his breath before second-thinking his response and leaning forward in the seat. "If this Primalis virus is out there, we all have a problem; nothing can stop it. We need to leave. Get as far away from civilization as possible. Get to the mountains."

Gyles looked back at him. "You know we're a bit short on transportation; we can't get everyone out. So, I ask again—you and me—are we going to have a problem?"

"These people aren't our concern. We can't save them all, Sergeant; it's time to make the tough decisions." Howard exhaled and folded his hands back into his lap. "But, if we are here... no, Sergeant, *we* will not have a problem. I am willing to put your oversight in judgment behind us."

Gyles laughed and looked back to the front. "Well, that's good to know, Doctor."

Traveling down a blacktop road, they passed shuttered homes and tree-lined streets. It looked like an average rural neighborhood. Gyles spotted a dog sitting quietly on a street corner... a typical Monday morning in rural America. Looking up, he knew that was an illusion. The midmorning sky between the treetops was speckled with black smoke, remnants of the burning gas station. Jones pulled the Humvee into an intersection. With the vehicle's engine idling, they could hear the popcorn crackle of rifle fire.

Jones looked to the sergeant. "Police station is north, at the end of Main Street. Left turn here and it's two stoplights to downtown, end of the line at a T-junction. Once there, right goes back to the highway and left is the national forest."

Gyles nodded and pulled his rifle close. He turned back and slapped the gunner's leg, who took the signal and stood over the M240 in the turret. "Okay, take us in easy," Gyles said. "Listen to my commands, and we'll be back at the ranch in no time."

"Sergeant?" Jones said. "That's the direction the shooting is coming from. Maybe the doctor is right; how 'bout we just turn around and head south? I know a place."

Gyles, not knowing the man enough to determine if it was sarcasm or cowardice, smiled. "Nah, maybe another time, Jones. Today is for killing, and the killing is up there."

Jones grimaced and gritted his teeth. He gripped the wheel tightly and mashed the gas pedal, letting the Humvee lurch forward and slowly pick up speed. Gyles checked the mirror and could see Weaver was following close behind in the tail vehicle, the truck's two gunners rotating and covering the right side and rear of the convoy.

Grassy dew covered the lawns of the well-kept homes. Cars sat parked in their driveways. At one point, Gyles thought he saw a curtain move from a window, revealing a woman's face as they raced by. The residential area changed to small-town commercial, the buildings spread out, with cars parked along the street. In the distance, he could see the glow of the burning gas station.

Before they made it to the next intersection, he saw them. They were still over two hundred meters ahead, in front of a blue house with its windows all broken and door removed from its hinges. An infected man was feasting over the body of a victim. The thing turned to face the noise of the approaching convoy and instantly became agitated.

The hideous monster turned out its lips like a dog, exposing blood-covered teeth. It screamed and howled at them, its hands tearing at its clothing. Another ran from a nearby yard. It arched its back and screamed with the other. More infected in the area were drawn to the blue house, all of them now excitedly looking at the approaching convoy. Gyles felt the vehicle pick up speed. He turned to Jones and could see the terror frozen on the man's face.

"Stay with me, Jones. Drive through the bastards. Stay straight—human or not, these things aren't getting through solid plate steel and ballistic glass," Gyles said. "Bump them off the brush guard, but do not put us into a tree! You got me?"

"I got you, Sergeant," Jones replied.

Gyles turned back and yelled to the gunner in the hatch. "Crazy sons o' bitches in the open, one hundred meters; let them have it!"

"Roger that. Contacts in the open, hundred meters, on the way!"

The big gun in the turret barked and Gyles watched as tracer rounds raced through the air at 2,800 feet per second. Like lasers, the rounds tore into the infected flesh, ripping the monsters apart. The creatures didn't make easy targets; once the first of them was knocked down, they scattered and sprinted on direct paths for the convoy.

Gyles saw intersecting fire as the angle increased, and the second truck's gunner joined the fight. Unarmored and running directly at the vehicles, infected crazies didn't stand a chance. Before the trucks passed the blue house, every one of the infected was in a crumpled mess, dead or dying.

As they passed the scene of carnage, Jones slowed down and Gyles fixed on one. What was once a female, had its body now contorted, its naked legs bent in an inhuman fashion. The creature looked at him with dead, rapidly blinking eyes. Gyles knew that the thing wanted to attack, but its body had been crippled by the 7.62 rounds that destroyed its spinal column. He leaned out of the window and carefully took aim with his carbine. He fired twice, hitting the top of the creature's head with the second shot.

"None of this makes sense," Howard shouted from the back, having witnessed the full assault. "It's supposed to be a virus. I don't know what this is. It's not...not... this is like a science fiction-style mutant weapon. Their actions, the anger, the rage... this is thousands of years of backward evolution in a matter of hours. I mean, I read the reports, but seeing it—it's just not possible."

"Not what you were expecting, Doc?" Gyles replied.

"Hell, no. Why would anyone do this? You can't create shit like this by accident! This is stuff designed in a nightmare factory—to destroy the part of the brain that makes us human but still preserve the ability to be a raving lunatic."

The Humvee slowed. "Sarnt? We're here." Gyles looked up; ahead was a roadblock that would make any combat veteran proud. Two black-painted Mine Resistant Ambush Protected (MRAP) vehicles with *Vines City Sheriff's Department* stenciled in white on the side in block letters were parked at forty-five-degree angles. The roadway to their front was covered with gator tail spike strips and rolls of concertina wire. A man was kneeling on the left MRAP, armed with a carbine, and a man with an oversized scoped rifle crouched on the vehicle to the right.

The station was positioned at a T-shaped intersection. Tall and made of red brick, the building was positioned behind the roadblock. The officers were facing toward the city with the roads coming in from the left and right, completely barricaded by wire and abandoned cars. Just as Gyles was trying to figure out how to approach, two uniformed men ran from the cover and pulled back the wire and gator strips.

The MRAP on the right backed up just enough to allow them through. Before Gyles could give the order, the policemen out front were yelling at them to proceed ahead. Without having to be told twice, Jones edged the Humvee through the gap that was closed as soon as they entered.

A short female dressed head-to-toe in black SWAT body armor approached Gyles's window. She had shoulders so broad Gyles couldn't tell if they were muscle or the firmness of the body armor. The woman tapped the glass with the back of a Maglite, grabbing his attention. Gyles released the combat lock, swung the door open, and joined her behind the hasty barricades. A rifle boomed from the top of an MRAP as more gunfire erupted on the opposite side.

"Damn, we can't ever get a break down here. It's about time the cavalry showed up," the woman yelled over the gunshots. She looked behind her to see the incoming assault of a half dozen infected. Seeing that her men had it under control, she looked back at Gyles. "I'm Sheriff Jenny Weber." She paused and looked at the sergeant's stone expression and at the pair of vehicles behind him. "We can really use the help." She stopped and looked at the pair of HUMVEEs. "Wait, how many you got with you?"

"Not enough. I'm Sergeant First Class Robert Gyles," he said, moving away from the vehicle to examine the hasty perimeter around the intersection. Bodies were hanging in spools of wire on both flanks; more dead were lying mangled in the streets nearby. From the road to the right, a pack of the infected rushed at them, breaking out of the shadows of a tree line, racing ahead like they were on fire, screaming and arms swinging. Gyles's turret gunner rotated into position and, with three quick bursts, stopped the attack. "You've been busy," Gyles said.

"Yeah, it's been a long watch. We'll see more of them; they've been coming like this all morning," Jenny said. "Most are coming from 81—the interstate to the east. We tried to patrol out that way early on just after the radios dropped, but it's a madhouse just five miles from here.

Gyles pointed to the bodies. "Who are they? Where are they coming from?"

"Best my man could tell, they're people trying to evacuate from the North and East, Washington D.C. mostly, but some even further." Jenny reached down for a small shoebox and pulled a wallet from inside it. Flipping back the leather fold, she displayed a Maryland driver's license. "All the way from Baltimore. Whatever the news said is going on to the north is spreading, and it's spreading fast. People are desperate to get away from it."

He took the ID from her and examined it. "When did you find this?"

"One of the first ones we found. I have it in a cell downstairs."

"It?" Gyles asked.

Howard approached from the shadows, interrupting. "Wait, you captured one? Alive? Are you sure it has the virus?"

Jenny paused, looking at the young doctor. Gyles looked at Howard then handed him the wallet and driver's license. "This is our medical expert, Doctor Howard."

Jenny nodded. "Yeah, we know he was infected. When my deputy found him, he was on the road having a seizure. My guy attempted to get him to a hospital, but he turned violent in the back of his patrol car. If it wasn't for the safety cage, he would have killed my deputy."

"But the patient... he's alive?" Howard asked again.

"Patient? You mean 'monster.' Hell no, it isn't alive. We put that thing down. There was no way to get the crazy bastard out of the patrol car. Tasers, pepper spray, none had any effect on it. I don't know if you've had an up-close look at these things but... they aren't keen on cooperation; they don't even communicate, other than screaming."

Howard shook his head and looked up toward a clearing sky. "All the way from Baltimore... The incubation period is more than we suspected. That means they could be halfway across the country by now... This is bad, the longer the incubation period, the more an injured person could travel before realizing it. Road blocks, checkpoints—none of that will work."

Jenny interrupted, holding up her hand. "So how long until we can evacuate the town?"

Gyles looked back at the sheriff. "I'm sorry, but you've got the wrong impression. We aren't a rescue mission; we came to *you* for help."

"How are we supposed to help you? Ya'll look in decent shape. You're from the armory, right?"

"Fort Stewart. We got kinda sidetracked at the armory." Gyles's eyes wandered the ground. Spotting the olive-drab ammo cans, he pointed and said, "That's what we need."

"The Army needs bullets? Since when?"

The sergeant nodded. "We used up most of our combat load this morning. I don't think we can last much longer if we aren't resupplied." Gyles looked up, seeing a tall black man in tactical SWAT body armor move across the top of the MRAP, carrying a large scoped AR-10 rifle. On his head was a woodland camouflage USMC ballcap and around his neck, a tightly tied shemagh. The man dropped heavily to the ground next to Jenny.

He looked at Gyles and the armored vehicles. "How many soldiers you got at the armory? What kind of equipment?"

"Excuse me?" Gyles asked, looking the man up and down.

"You asked for help. I need to know what you have to offer in return before we agree," he said mockingly. "If you can't help us, we need to balance our investment. You have no authority here."

Howard laughed. "The President has declared a national emergency and martial law. We don't need permission; we can take what we need. Asking was just a courtesy."

Gyles put a hand up, waving Howard off. "Okay, hold up, cowboy. I'm sure there is enough hate to go around without us having to start more among ourselves."

Stepping between them, Jenny said, "This is Luke, one of my deputies. I think what he's trying to say is you owe us some answers."

Nodding, the black man grinned, pulled a rag from

his pocket, and wiped sweat from his forehead. "Okay, Army, so what's going on? We know this isn't a civil war like GNN reported all last night. Is this the zombie apocalypse, or not?"

"Full-blown Armageddon, best I can figure," Gyles answered. "And my doctor here tends to agree."

Luke held a stiff expression and let his eyes shift from Gyles to Howard and back again. "You're serious."

Gyles sighed and locked eyes on the deputy. "Look, we don't have time for this shit. We need to consolidate our forces. You've done good out here, but when those things come in numbers, this flimsy wire won't do shit to hold them back. I've seen it and barely lived through it myself."

"And what do you suggest?" Luke asked.

Gyles looked at Jenny. She waved a hand. "Luke is my tactical expert; I defer to him."

"We load up everything you got and get back to the armory," Gyles said. "Hold out there, hope that help comes for us before the infected do."

"And what about the town?" Jenny asked. "We still have people here that need saving."

"I don't know about that. We tried going door to door earlier." Luke shook his head. "If what they are saying is true, the town is already lost."

"We can't just abandon them," Jenny retorted.

"No, that's not what I was suggesting. It's just unless they come to us, we can't risk losing more men to go after them," Luke said. "Listen, I'll stay back here with the MRAP and patrol the streets for as long as I can. I'll set up an observation post down the hill from the armory, and if I see survivors I can send them that way."

Gyles looked back at his men and turned to the sun making its way toward its apex. "I'll lend you two of my shooters. But listen, if you see a parade headed to town, you need to beat feet to the gates. If we get swarmed, we won't be able to let you in. And we sure as hell won't be able to help you."

Luke laughed. "Bro, this is an MRAP; I got food and water on board for two weeks. If we get swarmed, you'll be begging *me* to come inside, not the other way around."

CHAPTER NINE

Vines City Police Department.

With the convoy back online, they left the police barricade. Gyles watched through the rear window as the black MRAP pulled away and followed them, leaving the other MRAP alone at the roadblock. Luke gave them a wave before dropping into the armored vehicle and securing the hatch. Jenny, seated behind him in the Humvee, keyed a handheld radio and performed a quick radio check with Luke before placing it back into a pocket on her chest armor.

The ride through the small town revealed its devastation. Along Main Street, glass from shattered storefront windows littered the gore-covered sidewalks. In residential areas, front doors hung open and bodies lay in yards. Vehicles sat dead in the streets, many with broken windshields and windows, their occupants missing or dead.

Jenny stared ahead, her eyes frozen, her lower jaw trembling. "I tried to stop it. I sent four deputies into town over the last twenty-four hours; none came back," she said in a low cracking voice. "If it wasn't for Luke getting me straight, we would have lost the station too."

"You didn't know what was happening. How could you?" Gyles asked.

She shook her head. "We knew something was going on, just not what. The state police called it in just after midnight, said there was a lot of southbound traffic on the interstate, many accidents, and a sudden increase in violence. They told us it was panicked civilians getting away from the outbreak in Washington. We'd already heard a little bit about the guard boys up at the armory being recalled, so I took the warning seriously. They asked if we could provide some assistance in managing the traffic along the interstate exits closest to us.

"Tom, my deputy, volunteered to head out toward the highway and block the on-ramp. That's how he found the Baltimore man. He'd plowed into a tree in a single car accident off the side of 81. The guy was really messed up... broken jaw, broken arms, seizures. Tom called for an ambulance, but nobody was coming. He asked to take the injured man south, drive him to the hospital himself. I agreed, but he stalled out when he found both lanes were congested with people fleeing from the north. He really wanted to get some help for that man." She paused and took several deep breaths. "I ordered him back here.

"I knew something was off when the road into town backed up. We don't get traffic like that this late in the summer. This is Vines City, population five hundred. If it wasn't for the armory, this place wouldn't even be on the map—hell, even with the armory, it isn't on most maps. People only stop in this town for gas on the way to the national forest—" She stopped, looking ahead to the still-burning station. A charred firetruck was a part of the flames, and a Vines City patrol car sat empty with the driver door open.

"When that happened"—she pointed toward the fire—"I should have pulled everyone back. Hell, maybe I should have just sent them home and closed the station. Cut them loose, told everyone to get out of town ... maybe they'd still be alive. Their families would still have a chance."

"You couldn't have known," Gyles said again, having no other response.

"I should have known. The way that man from Baltimore acted when he finally woke up in the back of Tom's patrol car, the mixed radio reports about the riots and spread of infection... I should have known. Luke knew. I think in some way even Tom knew. Luke knew as soon as he saw the man, told me I needed to lock down the intersection, but still I waited." Her eyes filled with tears and she looked away. "I still sent out the damn patrols. I allowed the volunteer firefighters to respond to the station. I let traffic through. I let this happen! I'm responsible for all of it."

"It's in the past; none of that matters now," Gyles said.

She shook her head and turned toward the window. "They came just after three in the morning. A few at first, but before we could react, the phones were off the hook, people begging for help. We aren't a big department; the only reason I have as many officers as I do is because of all the rural homes and cabins close to the national forest. I just didn't have the people to respond to every call. We had to listen to people being attacked while they waited on the phone, screaming for help... they died waiting for help that wouldn't come.

"I had men down all over town and no way to back them up. They called for backup, and I had nobody to send. The state and county police went offline just after the first attacks. Luke finally insisted that we button up and block the roads, to recall all the reserve deputies. I didn't know what else to do... in twenty years, I've never seen anything like this."

"We've all seen a lot of firsts today." Trying to change the focus of conversation, Gyles said, "Who is he, this Luke? He seems to have his shit in one box."

She furled her lip. "Luke? He's a local boy; guess he's our sleepy town's very own war hero. He went off to the Marines after high school. He came back here and swore he was retired, but we managed to talk him into taking a part-time job with the department. He sort of works as our armorer. Does a lot of range training with us. Helps out in the summer when we get bogged down with tourists."

"What did he do? With the Marines, I mean."

"Not a hundred percent sure. He said he was a scout; well, he never said it, but that's what the tattoo says. He doesn't talk much about his time in the service. But he's a good man. He knows his stuff. My husband trusted him."

"Your husband?"

Jenny gritted her teeth and closed her eyes, turning back toward the passenger window. "Tom... he was the deputy that brought in the man from Baltimore," she said, her voice breaking and trailing off.

"Was he infected?" Howard asked her, speaking for the first time since leaving the barricade.

"Yeah," she whispered. "He didn't notice the scratch at first, but he felt it coming on... the shakes and the vomiting. Purple streaking around the wound. He left us... I know he took care of it so no one else would have to. He didn't even say goodbye. He just left."

"He was right to do it," Howard said. "There's no cure; there's just no coming back from it."

She nodded her head in agreement, looking at the doctor before covering her face so the men couldn't see her grief. "Tom was always like that... putting everyone else first."

The men remained silent, not knowing what to say. When the armory gates appeared to their front, the vehicle slowed. Gyles watched as two of his soldiers unchained the entrance and rolled back the gate, allowing the trucks to enter. Gyles opened the door and dismounted, letting the others gather around him.

He could see that the fortifications were complete; more wire had been strung along the perimeter fencing, men were positioned on the roof of the steel hangar, and others had dug in on the inside corners of the fence. Soldiers opened the back of the MRAP and began unloading cans of ammunition.

Gyles turned and saw Colonel Jessup approaching. The colonel stretched out his hand to Jenny. "Sheriff Weber, good to see you."

She took his hand and nodded without responding. Jessup turned back to Gyles. "Things are getting worse. We lost the news networks. Everything crashed about an hour ago—power, TV, Internet... all of it. We just switched to backup generators. They'll stay cranking out juice as long as we have natural gas."

"Any word from command?" Gyles asked.

"Nothing. We're on our own."

Gyles frowned. "What does that mean, exactly?"

"It's over... they're evacuating all the government leaders to secure locations. They've lit the fuse on something they're calling Operation Hecatomb."

Howard moved ahead quickly. "Excuse me, Colonel, did you say Hecatomb?"

"Ahh, Doctor Howard, is it? Glad you could join us. Yes, they say Operation Hecatomb. Are you familiar with it?"

The color drained from Howard's face. "We can't stay here."

"Details, Lieutenant," Jessup said, his face turning

hard. "If you know something, son, now is not the time to keep it to yourself."

"Operation Hecatomb is a highly classified CDC contingency plan; it literally means sacrifice. If they transmitted that word over the open radio net, then it's a go. Its sole design is to stop the spread of a virus... and stop it at all costs. Sure, on paper there are caveats to limit civilian casualties, but that's not the objective and won't stop them from completing the mission's purpose. Civilians are carriers and contribute to the spread, if they are moving toward a hard site, they will be considered legitimate targets.

"Sir, if they've really started Hecatomb, it means the virus has now spread out of control, beyond the containment lines drawn up by the CDC. They will begin firebombing heavy concentrations of infected areas. They will sacrifice large populations to spare others. The military will make last-ditch efforts to secure some of the large cities not affected by infection; they'll cordon off and close highways." Howard frowned then shook his head. "No... I imagine that has already failed. They'll pull back to remote locations and dig in."

Jessup's brow tightened and a hand drifted to massage the back of his neck. "What do you think, Sergeant?"

"I can't get you all out," Gyles said pointedly. He looked back at the trucks. "Even with every bit of armor and the Chinook, we'd still be leaving half of our people behind. If the sheriff knows a place, I'll keep the soldiers here and hold the fort while they evacuate. You can take the trucks, load up as many as you can, leave us here on foot. Maybe you can get all of the women and children out at least."

Jenny set her jaw. "And go where? To some remote farm, or a cabin in the mountains? And what do I do with a convoy full of women and kids and no soldiers to protect them when we get there?" she said. "I don't think we'll find anything better than this."

A cacophony of gunfire echoed in the distance— the distinctive crack of Luke's AR-10. "Sergeant, they're coming!" a soldier from the gate yelled. "There are a lot of them." High-pitched, feverish screams added to the urgency of the soldier's voice.

Gyles gritted his teeth and turned to Jessup. "Get inside and secure the building best you can. Lock us out and don't come looking for us; if we need something, we will come to you." He grabbed the sheriff by the shoulder. "Take your people inside with the colonel. Hold the entryways. Nothing gets inside; there are civilians in there. Your officers' priority is to protect them. If you must fall back, go to the roof and barricade the stairs."

Jenny shook her head, removed her cap, and pulled thick brown hair away from her forehead. She looked at him with concerned eyes. "Come inside with us."

"No." Pushing Howard ahead of him, he said, "But take my doctor. My men and I will stay out here. This is what we do."

She reached into a pouch on the back of her vest and handed him a Motorola radio. "Take this. If you need help, call."

"Likewise," Gyles said.

CHAPTER TEN

The Vineyards National Guard Armory Vines,
Virginia.

G yles looked over Weaver's shoulder at the newly
acquired police MRAP, which towered above
them to their rear. His machine gunner was inside the
open turret. Other men lay on the massive vehicle's
roof, taking advantage of the high vantage point. He
could hear the second MRAP fighting somewhere in
town; from the sounds, it was still some distance away.

At the bottom of the hill, shadowy shapes moved in
the trees, shifting among the thick foliage on the edges
of the blacktop road. Weaver, who knelt behind the
barrier of sandbags and earth in the corner of the
compound, pointed to an advancing group of infected.
They clung to the shoulders of the blacktop road that
wended down the hill to the main street. Some moved
as close as the large overflow parking lot before disap-

pearing among the vehicles less than a football field away. They stalked in tight groups, staying out of sight. Or at least attempting to.

"We should have cleared that parking lot out," Gyles said, keeping his eye to the optics. "We left them a place to hide."

"Fuck it. If it gets hairy, I'll put a mag full of red tips into those vehicles' gas tanks. Let the bastards cook," Weaver grunted.

Gyles laughed the way soldiers staring at death often do. "I like the way you think. Pull everyone up to this fence line except a small team and a gun truck on the back approach for rear watch."

"Already done, boss," Weaver whispered.

The sergeant grimaced and spoke loud enough so that the gunner on the MRAP could hear him. "If they break the cover on that lot, light their asses up. We have to keep them off the fence so the MRAP can get through."

"What about us?" a soldier to his right asked. Gyles looked at the young private. Unlike the rest of his men armed with M4 carbines and advance optics, this soldier carried an older model M16. Gyles knew he was one of the armory's men. He looked barely out of high school and scared to death.

"No, not you. I want you to hold your fire. Do not shoot unless something breaks through and gets to our immediate front. Your job is to protect the fence and gate security. Keep everything off it, shoot them right in the face from feet away—can you do that?"

The soldier stared at him with frightened eyes before swallowing hard and nodding his head. "Yes, Sergeant," he said, turning back to the front.

Gyles heard the distant MRAP growing closer, the sounds of the AR-10 barking louder with every second. In the tall grass to the front, he could see them moving. In single file, the things formed a column, the grass shifting with their movements as they approached in an ant-like formation in search of prey. Gyles watched as one of them broke cover and darted across an open space, seeming to fear the lack of concealment. Not as brazen as they were in the cover of darkness, they acted differently in daylight.

A quick burst from the gunner in the MRAP turret, and the sprinting man tumbled forward. Like firing a starter's pistol, the infected emerged from cover all along their front. For every one Gyles thought he'd spotted earlier, at least ten more existed in the shadows of the trees.

They charged forward in a monstrous human wave. Screaming primal roars from their rage-filled faces, they advanced. Sickening cries and howls followed the human wave. The machine gunner on the MRAP went cyclic, spitting 7.62 rounds into the infected swarm at a rate of 500 rounds per minute. The mass was shredded in the open, the infected eventually drifting into the cover of the parking lot but not quitting. Weaver pushed up to a knee and loaded the magazine from his vest filled with tracer rounds. Firing in semi-auto, he pumped shots into the space just behind the cab of a large pickup truck. After five shots, the Ford truck burst into flames. Not stopping, Weaver shifted fire to an SUV on the far side of the lot. Soon, the parking area was an inferno of black roiling smoke and screaming infected.

The creatures howled, running at the fence with their clothing engulfed in flames. They broke through the last of the overgrown grass and spread out, running for the compound gates. Gyles raised his own rifle and fired two well-placed shots into the face of a stocky man. Signaling with his own gunfire, the men who were dug into the base of the fence joined in, knocking down the last of the advancing monsters. Gyles looked up from his optics; the field to the front was clear, nothing remained on its feet. At the base of the hill, he spotted a blur of motion. The second MRAP was racing up the narrow street and turning onto the base access road.

The armored vehicle's front grill was covered in gore. Dead creatures clung to the sides in grotesque death grips. Parts of bodies hardly recognizable as human were ground into the fenders and treads of the large vehicle. Without slowing, the black armored truck raced to the gate and screeched to a stop. A helmeted head popped from the roof-mounted turret. "Open the gate!" Luke screamed. "I got shit loads of hungry bastards on my ass!"

Two soldiers emerged from cover and fumbled with the gate lock. The M240 from the parked truck opened again, the machine gunner firing into a new approaching mass. Gyles stood and walked to the side to see. A horde was pouring around the corner, headed to the access road. Luke was in the turret of his own vehicle; facing back, he fired and shot as the gate was opened and the MRAP pulled through. "Close it, close it," soldiers screamed while others frantically fumbled with the lock.

As soon as the vehicle was through, Luke climbed onto the roof and stood with his feet planted. The big rifle to his shoulder, he continued firing into the advancing mob. Gyles watched the things swarm forward up the armory access road. Unlike before, this group was in a full charge. They were enraged and out for blood, not looking for cover. For every row of them that fell into the dirt, riddled with bullets, more fought their way into the opening, eager to get their chance at the soldiers at the top of the hill.

With all their weapons now online and working together, the mob was quickly cut down. It wasn't a fight; it was an organized slaughter, but at the cost of hundreds of precious rounds of ammunition. A Squad Automatic Weapon gave a final burst before the men's weapons fell silent. Gyles stood and approached the fence, taking account of the space to their front. Men called out for ammo as soldiers ferried green bandoleers of ammunition. Luke dropped down from the truck and stepped close. "Where's the sheriff?"

"Holding the fort inside," Gyles said, pointing to the steel hangar. He looked at the Marine. His face held a clean scar that ran across his forehead that he hadn't noticed before, and, as Jenny had noted, the man wore a scoped, crossed rifle tattoo on the side of his neck, the words *Scout* written below it.

Luke reached into a chest rig and removed a bottle of water. He spun the cap and drank until it was empty. "We were heading down the road, decided to come back up here when we spotted them behind and in front of us. For a second, I thought maybe you all might be gone, that we'd be stuck all alone out there."

Weaver laughed and leaned against the fence. "Alone? Could be worse, you could be up here standing between those things and a hundred civilians inside."

"A hundred? You are shitting me." Crushing the remains of the plastic bottle, Luke looked around him. "There'll be more, lots more. I saw three times this many on the county access road; it's only a matter of time until they find us."

"How'd it look out there?" Gyles asked. "Any survivors?"

Luke shook his head. "We stayed at the roadblock for about an hour. They started coming down the eastern road from the interstate. I took out the first dozen, then we buttoned up. The things just kept coming." Luke dug through a pocket on his sleeve, finding a pack of cigarettes. He dug one out and lit it with an old lighter. Luke sucked in the poison then exhaled; he pointed his cigarette at the stacks of the dead outside the gates. "There aren't this many people in the whole damn county. I don't know, maybe the gunfire is drawing them here."

Gyles shrugged. "Not like we can prevent that."

"Maybe I should go back out, make some serious noise, and try to pull them away."

The sergeant shook his head. "Negative. These things are moving in packs; you might lead one away, but two more will find their way to us. That pack we killed earlier was here before you."

Luke nodded. "Then let them come to us." He dropped the cigarette and snuffed it with the heel of his boot. "Where do you want me then?"

Pointing to the large-bore rifle clipped to the man's chest, Gyles asked, "How much food you got for that?"

Luke grinned, showing his white teeth. "Enough to feed an army."

"I could use a sniper on the roof."

"Fair enough; that's where you'll find me then."

CHAPTER ELEVEN

DAY OF INFECTION PLUS SEVEN, 1945 HOURS

The Vineyards National Guard Armory Vines, Virginia.

Gyles walked the fence line. His men were tired, lying behind their rifles, weary from the hours of adrenaline and living on the edge. Most of them were consuming the last of the food they'd brought in with them. It had been over twelve hours since they left Fort Stewart on a recovery mission that should have lasted three. Since the last attack, the hillside had been quiet. No signs of activity, but Gyles knew they were down there, somewhere in Vines City, or traveling the road leading from the interstate. He walked toward the back of the compound to check the overgrown fields to their rear.

He felt her move behind him. He spun to see Jenny approaching, holding a Styrofoam cup. She handed it off to Gyles, who grinned, breathing in the hot coffee before sipping at it. "You don't know how badly I needed this," he said.

"You should come inside and get some rest."

"I'll catch a nap out here once I finish my rounds. If you have officers to spare, my men could use a break. Would your people mind sitting the wall for a spell?"

"They'd love to; they're going crazy inside," she said, looking at the distant tree line, the sun hovering just above the treetops. "You know it'll be dark soon."

"Then we'll kill them in the dark."

She stepped closer and looked around to make sure nobody else was within earshot. "Have you thought about what we'll do if they break through?"

"If they get inside, I don't think there is much we can do. I'll have the boys saddle up in the armored vehicles, and we will hold them off for as long as we can, but after that?" He shrugged.

"You don't sugarcoat it, do you?"

"A sweet turd wouldn't be any easier to swallow."

She dipped her chin and followed him to the rear perimeter fence. Tall grass swayed in the wind, large swaths of the field covered in shadows of the swiftly dropping sun. Gyles looked at the weak parts in the perimeter fence, blind spots that were hard to cover. They didn't have men to patrol back there, and they didn't have claymores, but Luke had used the down time to string up a case of flash bang grenades to trip wires along the weak areas of the fence. They wouldn't do much damage, but they'd at least alert the soldiers to an attack at their backs.

Jenny pointed to a distant hilltop. "The national forest is just on the other side."

"I've never been," Gyles said.

"Maybe when this is over?"

Gyles shook his head. Looking at the hill, he froze and focused on the distant fields to his front. Something tingled in the back of his brain. He thought he saw the tops of the tall grass moving; it swayed unevenly against the grain of the subtle breeze. Jenny noticed his change in posture and took a step back. "Do you see something?" she asked.

Gyles held a finger to his lips. Some two hundred yards out, a flock of birds cackled and flew into the air. The grass seemed to wave at him, like the ripple of moving water, the bending blades catching the final rays of the sun. When more birds flew into the air, this time just a hundred yards to his front, he knelt and brought up his rifle. "We're in trouble."

She leaned in. "What can I do?"

"Get Sergeant Weaver; get him back here now." Gyles took a deep breath, keeping his eye on the optics. He focused on the dark texture of the waves, panning his sight to a low spot in the terrain where the ground was uneven and brown. A natural opening in the pasture, it was a place where water had once settled and stunted the growth of the grass. Gyles closed his eyes tightly, trying to relax and control his breathing. When he opened them, the glowing dot in his optic was centered on the face of a demon.

The creature's eyes looked like black marbles

against the setting sun. As Gyles focused on the thing's head, another dozen emerged from the tall grass around it, all of them crouched like a pack of wolves on the hunt. His heart beat out of his chest as his finger caressed the trigger, his thumb pushing down on the selector switch. He tried to calm himself and wait for back up. He didn't want to initiate contact alone. If they rushed the fence, he wouldn't be able to hold them all.

The monster to his front paused then put its nose to the air like a dog sniffing out its prey. It chewed and licked like it could taste their scent. Gyles wondered if their primal sense evolved as others degraded. As they became wilder, losing the ability to reason, did they gain more in the ability to hunt and kill? Gyles thought the infected man looked back and locked eyes with him. He knew it was impossible; he was kneeling in the shadows of the fence. The creature couldn't see him.

He waited, counting down the precious seconds. More of the monsters entered the clearing. They would be across it soon, and then he wouldn't have another clear shot until they reached the fence. It was now or never. Gyles aimed at the sweet spot just below the creature's chin. He held his breath and took the slack out of the trigger. As his own rifle bucked, he heard the report of automatic weapons fire from the front of the compound, then more gunshots to his right. Quickly he realized he was alone, yet all his men were engaged. *No, they're attacking on all sides*, Gyles thought to himself.

Gyles focused to his front and saw the creatures were no longer prowling. With the gunfire enraging them, they were now sprinting forward in the tall grass like a herd of African gazelles in the setting sun. Fear filled his chest; there were more attacking than he had ammo on his person. But he was a warrior; he had no qualms about his responsibility. He would die here holding the line if he had to. He fired until the bolt locked back on his rifle. As he reloaded, the faces of the children in the hangar filled his thoughts. His heart grew heavy with torment.

He thought of his parents, his siblings, his high school football coach, a friend he'd left behind in the sands of Iraq. How many of them would be ashamed of his failure on this far-off hill in the middle of nowhere? How many families would he let down by failing to hold this position? He sucked in hate and exhaled discontent as he locked his sights on the mass to his front, shouting obscenities as he fired into their already broken bodies.

A bright flash and boom blinded him. A flash bang less than fifty feet to his right had been triggered. He could feel the heat on his face. His head felt crushed and ringing filled his ears as the concussion nearly knocked off his helmet. He shook the stars from his vision, hearing the clanging of bodies against the fence. When he looked back, they were on the wire to his front. Violent explosions thundered against his skull as the daisy-chained string of flash bangs triggered up and down the fence line. His vision clouded with bright spots, but he forced his eyes ahead, fighting the closing in of his vision.

He screamed, not hearing his own words over the ringing in his ears and fired directly into the creatures above him. Bile filed his mouth, his stomach rebelling against the spinning in his head. The infected madly climbed the fence, becoming entangled in the wire, screaming at him as their flesh ripped against the razor wire.

He tumbled and fell onto to his back, continuing to fire madly at the horrifying sight above him while screaming back at the monsters incoherently. Weaver ran to his side with other men close by. They put their own weapons into the fight. But even with all of the combined firing, the fence was giving; it was collapsing inward, the poles bending. "We have to pull back!" Weaver yelled.

"There is nowhere to pull back to!" Gyles shouted. "We fight here, or we die here!"

There was a roar of an engine and blasting of a horn. Gyles rolled out of the way just as the MRAP raced through and pressed against one of the supports. The driver used the mass of the vehicle to push against the waves of infected, righting the fence while the turret gunner fired point-blank into the faces of the infected. Wind whipped around him; the Chinook was spinning up, slowly climbing into the air and rotating clockwise. The door gunners lit fire to the chain guns on either side, erasing large streaks of the infected as they stormed the fences. They weren't stopping; no matter how much they fired, the infected still came. They didn't care how many of their own were killed. They had a single focus—to get at the people inside the fence.

Gyles was feeling the effects of the concussion grenades, the blood rushing from his head. His arms felt heavy. He was falling back, fighting the urge to close his eyes. He went weak and collapsed to the ground. Weaver caught him by the back of his armor and began dragging him back to the building. Gyles tried to resist but had no strength in his legs, his arms as heavy as concrete. He pulled in his rifle tight with everything he had. Raising his weapon, he fired into the infected-filled fences as he was dragged helplessly along the tarmac. Finally, Weaver pushed him into a seated position, and he felt his men crowding in beside him.

The outer fences were failing, and the creatures were spilling over the tops. The mounted guns on the armored vehicles were cutting down the monsters as they fell over the concertina wire, looping and hanging from torn flesh. The Chinook orbited, using its chain guns to try to stop the advance. Gyles was dizzy, but even in a drunken mind, he knew the Chinook's guns would run dry or suffer from warped barrels before they put down the assault. The compound was going to be overrun. It was going to fall, and he didn't know what to do.

Gyles pushed back against the men supporting him

and looked at the hangar door. "We have to get inside," he shouted.

Weaver nodded his head, acknowledging him. He pulled his platoon sergeant to his feet then, together, they turned and charged toward the hangar. With less than ten feet left to travel, the door exploded out as civilians rushed onto the tarmac. Gyles screamed for them to stop, but the panicked people flooded out. Gyles could see the muzzle flashes of weapons being fired inside the darkened space. Before his men could focus and provide relief to the fighting inside, infected creatures streamed out of the hangar entrance, chasing the civilians.

A large man covered in gore flew through the air, pouncing on a woman's back. She screamed and collapsed to the ground with the enraged man tearing a large strip of flesh from the back of her neck. A soldier screamed as he charged head-on into the madness, firing his rifle point-blank into the escaping horde. Gyles watched the soldier get swatted aside. As the man's twisted body fell, he recognized the young soldier as Corporal Jones, the local trooper he'd forced on the convoy into town.

Gyles stepped back, stunned; they were all dying... all his men were dying. Gunfire all around him now, his hearing was a symphony of high-pitched buzzing and bursts of static. The sun had fallen, the air filled with smoke and strobes of muzzle flashes. He'd lost control. His men were no longer fighting as a team. Survival instinct had taken over. He watched as an armored Humvee with the hatches secured crashed the front gate, bouncing the infected off its hood as it fled the compound and raced down the approach road. Another truck made laps around the tarmac, crushing creatures under its huge tires.

Gyles made a final push to reach the hangar, still flanked by Weaver and a pair of his soldiers. Finally reaching the doorway, he looked inside. He could see Jenny and a pair of the deputies backed into a corner, feverishly fighting against the wave of infected pouring out of the office area. As instructed, the colonel had barricaded the hallway entrance with office furniture. But it wasn't enough; the infected pressed through as if launched from a firehose.

He watched as a massive wave pushed the police officers against the wall, snapping jaws and screams overwhelming them. Changing magazines in his rifle, Gyles prepared to charge forward when he was tackled from behind. He rolled to his back to find a creature tearing at his armor, bloodied hands clawing at his vest, its teeth biting at the rim of his Kevlar helmet. The soldier shifted and struggled. Forcing the muzzle of his rifle into position, he pumped the trigger until the creature's body went limp.

He fought back to his feet. His friends around him were now all engaged in close combat. He spotted Weaver on the ground, tussling with a creature of his own. He ran forward, kicked the infected woman under the chin, and watched it lose its grip and fall back before he could level his rifle and shoot the thing in the face.

The battle in the hangar was lost, the outside perimeter overrun. Back on his feet, Weaver stepped back, the two men moving together. Gyles leveled his rifle at a pair of charging infected and fired until his weapon was empty, killing both. He reached for a reload and found his vest empty. Gyles drew his pistol and looked back at Weaver who'd already gone to his sidearm. The area surrounding them was madness.

The Chinook was still orbiting. Its guns dry, the bird was attempting to use its heavy rotor wash to hold back the waves of infected. Most of the armored vehicles were fighting their way out of the compound now, racing to join the others on the access road. Gyles pushed back, feeling Weaver directly behind him. "We're fucked, aren't we?" Weaver shouted.

"Depends how you look at it," Gyles said. "Work day is almost over."

Gyles focused on the gap in the fence; a mob was racing at him, running, pushing at each other to be the first to reach him, their gnarled faces dripping gore. He leveled his pistol, lined his eye up to the iron sights, and watched the creatures charge as the world seemed to freeze around him. Every hour of training, every engagement, every battle, now came down to this. They were all dead; his unit was gone, the people under his charge lost. All that was left was him pressed against his brother. Every shot counted. He fired and watched the head of a creature explode.

Shifting his focus, Gyles aimed and pulled the trigger. He no longer saw faces or features of the infected —he dropped all of that and thought of them as objects —objects out to destroy him. He pulled the trigger again, hitting one in the face. The slide locked back on his M9. His hand dropped to his hip to retrieve a reload, but he knew there wouldn't be time. They were moving too fast; they would be on him before he could fire again. He prepared for the impact.

With a blast, an MRAP crushed the remaining creatures and collided with the hangar door, forcing it shut. Steel screeched as the large vehicle backed away. Soldiers poured from the rear doors, one of them grabbing Gyles in a bear hug and carrying him to the back of the tall armored vehicle. Gyles struggled against the man. His body weak, he felt himself being thrown inside. The doors slammed shut, the screaming of the infected blocked out by the noise. Their claws scratched against the armored walls. The vehicle pulled away like an ice breaker moving through the sea of monsters.

"What the hell are you doing?" Gyles screamed, struggling to rise.

A man pulled at his collar and shook him. "It's okay, there's nothing left to do."

Gyles fought against the man's grip. "No! There're people back there. Let me out."

The man pressed his face close to his own. "Look at me, Sergeant. It's me... Luke. There is nothing left; nothing we can do. It's over."

Gyles closed his eyes. His throat squeezing shut, he felt the tears on his cheeks. "It can't ...." he struggled to stay awake. The pressure in his head becoming unbearable, the torment in his thoughts screaming at him, he finally relented and let the darkness take him.

CHAPTER TWELVE

DAY OF INFECTION PLUS EIGHT, 0900 HOURS

GW National Forest, Virginia.

H is head jerked forward with the sudden stop of the HUMVEE. The sun was bright, shining in through the dirt-coated windshield. He turned his head wearily and gazed out into the open desert, looking closer at the debris-covered shoulder of the road. Plastic bottles, cardboard, garbage bags, even dead animals littered the roadside. He was hot, and his head hurt. He could feel the sweat rolling down his temples. He removed his glove and put his hand over the barely cool air coming from the returns.

"Why are we stopped?" he asked.

Before anyone could answer, the radio came alive with chatter. The driver put the handset to his ear and looked back at him. "They want you at the front of the convoy, Sergeant Gyles."

Gyles focused on the driver's face; he knew the

man's eyes, but he couldn't come up with the name. He cursed himself for falling asleep—he never slept on patrol. He nodded and opened his door, stepping into the blast furnace of the Iraqi desert.

The bright sunlight reflecting off the bleached surface of the road forced him to squint. He searched his pockets for his sunglasses, but they were gone. Again, he cursed and started the march ahead, every step hitting him like he was walking the surface of the sun. Ahead he saw the crowd; they were gathered around a deep crater in the center of the road. He closed his eyes again and slowly opened them. Colonel Jessup looked back at him and waved him forward. He moved closer then froze.

"Why is Jessup here?" he said aloud, then looked left and right to see that the road was empty, the convoy gone. Back to the front, the hole was still there, Jessup standing over its edge, Captain Younger beside him. They were waving Gyles forward. He didn't want to go, but his feet wouldn't stop. He approached the rim of the crater. Younger and Jessup placed hands on him, trying to push him in. Below in the hole, he could see the twisted and bloodied faces of his men, the civilians from the armory. They were writhing in pain screaming at him to help, trying to climb out of the hole.

"No, stop!" he screamed

He rolled hard and felt his body bounce off the hard floor, the revving of a diesel engine and the protesting of steel echoing in his ears. Gyles opened his eyes then immediately clenched them shut from the pain in his head. Slowly, he opened them again. He was in the back of an MRAP. He turned his head and could see boots and piles of gear on the floor beside him.

Gyles saw two sleeping men on the bench to the right, more across from them on the left. He looked at the gear strapped into the troop seats then at the ceiling. Ahead, he could see the driver and another in the passenger seat. He reached out and grabbed a strap, attempting to pull himself up. The strap was attached to a rucksack and it came down on top of him, spilling over an ammo can filled with loose rounds. He pushed the rucksack away and looked up to see Weaver staring down at him.

"Gawd damn, you're alive," Weaver shouted.

Gyles scowled and stuck out his hand for a lift. "Da fuck is that supposed to mean?"

Weaver reached down and helped lift his platoon sergeant up into one of the troop seats. Gyles leaned back and found it far more conformable than what he was used to. No canvas seat; instead they were black leather bucket seats. Weaver caught his stare and said, "Police get the vehicles from surplus, but they add things to make them better."

Gyles nodded and looked back to the front. He could see that they were on a gravel road, following a HUMVEE to their front. "We lost the armory, didn't we?" Gyles said.

Weaver nodded his head. "Yeah, I thought I lost

you too when you fell out after we got you into the battle wagon. You've been out almost twelve hours. The doctor thought maybe you were infected."

"Infected? Am I?" Gyles asked.

"No. The Doc says you have a concussion," Weaver said. "Probably from all those flash bangs bouncing off your grape. I don't know how you stayed conscious through that."

Gyles shook his head then looked to the pair of soldiers sleeping on the seats. His eyes swiveled past all the empty space. "This truck isn't full. How many did we lose?"

Weaver shook his head. "It's not good. We've got four HUMVEEs and the two MRAPS. Nineteen made it out, including the cops and National Guard guys."

"Including?" Gyles asked, not really wanting to know the answer.

"We have five troops from First Squad and two from Second. With us, plus the Doc, ten of us are all that's left of the platoon."

Gyles's stomach turned, and he thought he was going to be sick. They'd flown out of Fort Stewart with forty men. He leaned back and took a deep breath, accepting a water bottle Weaver handed him. After taking heavy drinks he said, "The Chinook?"

Weaver shrugged. "Not great news, but the best we got, if you can call it that. They were able to pull some people off the roof and get away. They tried for Belvoir." The man paused and looked back toward the windshield. "It's gone, Robert. The place was overrun; they had to turn back."

"Where are they?"

"National forest. It's where we're headed. Luke knows a spot that's about as remote as you can get. The bird landed there early this morning and reported the area unoccupied."

"No," Gyles said, leaning forward struggling to stand. "We need to go to D.C. That's where Captain Younger said the battalion and the rest of the division were headed."

Weaver put out a hand and guided him back down and into his seat. "You need to take it easy," he said. "We can't go to the Capital. Rose said the bombing has already started. The Air Force is knocking out bridges and highway overpasses and hitting large populations. We would never make it. Best thing to do right now is hunker down. The men are in no condition for a fight."

"The bird got to Belvoir, then just turned back? They couldn't find a safe place in D.C.? The Army didn't have a place for them?"

"The Capital is a warzone, boss. Rose said the city was under full assault on all sides. Anything flying is evacuating people while the troops on the ground fight it out. They had civilians on board, and the combat air controllers waved them off. Told them to dump their civilians and return to help with the extraction of government officials."

"Dump?"

"Yeah, that's what they said."

"Where?"

"They were given coordinates of a FEMA camp outside the city proper. When they flew over it, the place was nothing but bodies and blowing canvas. They called it in and were told to leave the families any place that looked hospitable. Rose said the pilots weren't interested in trading civilian lives for government cronies, so they cut off communications and came back to us."

"Where were the officials going?"

Weaver shrugged. "Some bunker complex in Colorado; they wouldn't give up the location."

The MRAP slowed and, looking up, Gyles could see that they were easing off the broken road and onto a graded path. Straining, he could see the eaves of rustic cabins and finally the outline of the CH-47 parked on the outer edge of a wide grass field. The truck stopped, and Luke looked back at him for the first time. The man didn't speak but gave him a frowning nod before opening the door and leaving the vehicle.

"Let's get out of here," Gyles said, pointing to the door.

Weaver leaned past him and worked a control, letting the rear ramp drop down. The bright light pouring in woke the troopers sleeping in the troop seats. Gyles shifted his weight and, taking a handhold on the ceiling, maneuvered himself out of the MRAP. He turned back, took a quick look, and spotted his rifle. He snatched it up then took simple steps forward, testing his balance. Weaver moved out beside him as Gyles surveyed the terrain.

They were at the end of a gravel road in a semi-circle. Ahead of them were three cabins—a large one in the center, flanked by two smaller ones. A field was off to the right with a pair of picnic pavilions, what he could only imagine were outhouses, and a large fire pit. The entire area was surrounded by tall, full trees. "Looks like a damn Boy Scout camp," he mumbled.

Weaver's eyes performed the same scan, and the man nodded his agreement.

Luke rounded the vehicle with the AR-10 held in his right hand and said, "Welcome back."

Gyles shook off the comment.

Luke gave a knowing half smile. "We are a day's drive up hard terrain from Vines. Even if they managed to follow us, it'll be at least a day or two before they get here."

Looking at the big cabin, he could see the door was open. A woman walked out, leading a pair of kids toward the outhouse. "How many dependents we got here?" Gyles asked.

"Nine, all women and kids. Came in with the Chinook."

"Shooters?"

Luke shrugged. "Including the five on the flight crew, two of my officers made it off the roof."

"The sheriff?"

Luke shook his head no.

Gyles exhaled through pursed lips. "These

numbers are making my head hurt. So what's the count? How many people do we have in camp?"

"Thirty-five."

Gyles scratched at his head. He saw the CH-47 pilots and Rose approaching his little circle. He waited for the flight crew to join his little pow-wow then he looked at Rose. "What's the status on the bird?"

Mitchell, the pilot, answered for his crew chief. "Grounded, we came in on fumes. We might get it in the air, but we have less than thirty minutes of flight time. Thirty is being generous though. I wouldn't count on more than ten. We're checking the maps; with any luck, we'll find a field close enough to top off."

Rubbing his temples, Gyles clenched his eyes shut. "If we stuff the Hummers full and max out the MRAPs with ten each, we can drive out of here then?" It was more a question than a statement.

Luke shook his head no. "Not so fast—we ran our vehicle tanks dry getting here. Those MRAPs are thirsty, and the armored Hummers aren't much better off. We have about twenty gallons of diesel in cans for the entire convoy. Not like we have a logistics train inbound to resupply us."

Gyles looked at Weaver, who shrugged, then at Rose, who shook his head.

"You make the call, Sergeant," Mitchell said.

"Give me the rundown on your summer camp here, Luke," Gyles said. "What am I looking at?"

Luke undid the Velcro on his black SWAT armor so it was hanging open on the sides. "Well, it's mostly out of use. I used to do some hunting and fishing over the next ridge line and would park my truck up here on longer trips." He stopped and pointed to the buildings. "Nobody stays here. I've never seen anyone hang out in the cabins more than a couple hours. I bumped into a park ranger a couple years back; he said this place used to have something to do with the Civilian Conservation Corps, then later it was used as billeting for workers that were sent up here to work on the roads and to cut timber inside the reservation."

"And now?" Gyles asked.

"Most I've ever seen is hikers stopping in for lunch, stuff like that. They usually stick to the pavilion and the BBQ grills. The big one is solid. The smaller cabins need some work, but they're well-built so it won't take much effort to really harden them up." He wiped sweat from his forehead as he looked at the structures. "They'll support our needs—short term at least."

"What are you thinking?" Gyles asked.

The man closed one eye and looked at the terrain then back to Gyles. "We can break down the plywood off the pavilion roofs to barricade the cabin windows. I know of a fence row not far from here; we can pull that up and cut trees to do the rest. There is no getting the civvies out of here, so I suggest we barricade and get safe. At least until someone can come for us or we figure out how to rustle up some fuel."

Staring at the building, Gyles pursed his lips, considering the options before he turned to Weaver. "What's the gauge on food and ammo?"

The man shook his head. "We burnt up a lot of ammo getting out of Vines. Food situation isn't quite as dire. We have plenty of MREs and water for a few days."

Again, looking at Luke, Gyles grinned. "This is your hunting ground? Can it provide for us?"

The man thought about it, then said, "I wouldn't want to fire a shot up here. It could pull those things to us; a gunshot can travel for miles." He paused, considering the question again. "I think I could work something on the river behind us, maybe rig some nets. But I wouldn't get excited about it; we have a lot of mouths to feed."

"Okay," Gyles said, keeping his eyes on the cabins. "You harden up the camp and do what you can to find some game. Your officers have control of the civilians." He looked to Rose. "Make sure the guys in green do what's needed to help here. I'll take a gun truck and the empty fuel cans with Sergeant Weaver and see what we can find out there. There has to be something close by."

The men nodded and broke off, returning to what they were doing. Weaver waited for them to leave earshot before he looked at his platoon sergeant. "We aren't going anywhere today. You need rest and so do the men. The guys are falling apart, and you aren't in much better shape. Look at you, ya can barely stand."

Gyles shook his head. "There's no time for that. I'm fine, and you know it."

"Take a break, Sarge, or this trip isn't going to

happen. I won't roll with you, and I'm not sending my people out with your head still full of cotton balls and cobwebs." Weaver pointed toward the main cabin building, where men were gathering to eat meals and drink from canteens. "Head up there and get some chow, and we'll talk again. Get some rest, boss."

Preparing to argue, Gyles took a step forward and felt the weight in his legs. He was light-headed from lack of food and the pounding headache. Each limb felt like it was wrapped in concrete blankets. He looked down at his watch. His men had been going non-stop for over thirty-six hours. His literal respite of unconsciousness in the back of the MRAP was the most rest he'd had since getting the call from Lieutenant Michaels nearly three days ago.

Gyles looked back up at Weaver and put a hand on his shoulder. "Thanks, brother. I appreciate you keeping me straight." He exhaled and looked toward the vehicles parked in a diagonal line along the front of the compound. "I'll take a couple hours. You get to the men and make sure they are rotating and doing the same."

Weaver nodded.

CHAPTER THIRTEEN

GW National Forest, Virginia.

Weaver had been right to force him down, to take a break and let the team lick its wounds. Once given the proper opportunity to rest, he realized how broken and bruised his team really was. For himself, what was supposed to be a few hours nap, turned into two days of downtime. His men were beaten worse than he originally thought, and no matter how much drive he thought he had, he couldn't clear the ringing in his own head. Still the time wasn't wasted. They dug in and improved the compound, using what they could to make them more comfortable.

Once he'd stripped out of his body armor and gear, he could see that there wasn't a spot on his flesh that didn't wear a dark bruise or a lump from the previous night's fight. He'd collapsed soon after. He'd slept nearly a full day before being woken once an hour by the medic to make sure he was still alive. Howard said he was certain it was a TBI (Traumatic Brain Injury), but without a brain scan there was no way to be sure. They would settle on a concussion and treat him accordingly. The voices, the questions about what he'd done wrong, all the second-guessing sat in the front of his mind. But his problems weren't just in his head.

He'd finally talked his way out of bedrest the evening before and now, after having a breakfast of fresh-caught fish and some weak coffee, he was feeling restless. His head was still pounding, and he knew it was about to get worse as he watched the unit's sole surviving medic, Specialist Rodriguez, walk his way.

The young man had come by to check on him, but mostly to give him a final exam to make sure he wasn't infected. Even though Doctor Howard was no longer in charge of the mission, or what was left of the people on it, he had managed to persuade and gain influence over the platoon medic. He was going from person to person, taking temperatures for fever and doing quick inspections for cuts and bites, which was recently determined to be the primary means of transmission of the infection.

When the medic got to him, Gyles wanted to bark and turn him away, but he looked at the faces of the other soldiers closely watching him. There was no bravado in denying treatment in the field, so he bit his tongue and went along with the exam. If he wanted the confidence of his men, he needed a clean bill of health. The medic was barely out of high school but having been on the battalion's tour to Iraq, he was far from green. Just over five foot, he had shoulders as wide as an Ox, and Gyles knew from firsthand experience the kid could be counted on in a fight. "No cuts, no bites, no scratches that I can see, Sergeant. Take these for the headaches, just one a day," Rodriguez said, handing Gyles three 800mg Ibuprofen pills. "I wish I could give you more."

Gyles put his uniform shirt back on. "Yeah, I gotcha," he said, making a mental note to look for medicine along with fuel, ammo, and food. "How are the rest of the men?"

"They are okay," Rodriguez said. "We could use some better chow though."

Nodding, Gyles forced a smile. "You're doing an excellent job. Keep an eye on them, and if anything changes, let me or Weaver know."

The medic nodded his head. He went to step away but stopped and turned back. "Sergeant, are you really going back out there?"

Gyles hardened his jaw. "We have to."

"Has there been any word from Fort Stewart?"

The platoon sergeant shook his head, not speaking. Rodriguez frowned. "Take the pills, Sergeant; they'll help with the headaches," he said before lowering his head and walking away.

Gyles dressed and lifted his IOTV (Improved Outer Tactical Vest). He removed the back and side ballistic plates, only leaving the one in the front before putting the vest back on. Most of the other soldiers had already made the change after Luke and Weaver suggested it. From what they'd seen, the infected weren't shooting back, and he remembered how cumbersome it had been fighting them in the heavy gear. Then, with his pack slung over his shoulders and rifle in hand, Gyles walked to the end of a small fenced-in quad.

Under Luke's supervision, they'd wasted no time hardening the three cabins into a mini compound. It wasn't fully walled, but they'd built spiked picket fences and trenches that surrounded the buildings. No need for fences that could be climbed like before— these fences were designed to impale. They'd learned their lesson the hard way at the armory. Now it was about holding the infected back so they could be killed.

The constructed defenses around the cabins looked medieval, more like a Dark Ages encampment than a modern military outpost. Sharpened stakes and picket lines with steel cables stretched between the trees had been designed to trip up runners and crowd the infected into firing lanes. If they managed to get beyond those, there were the trenches filled to slow them further. So far, they hadn't seen or heard anything in the way of infected, and they hoped it would stay that way. Gyles weaved his way through the barricades and moved to the narrow drive.

Weaver was already with one of the armored HUMVEEs when Gyles approached it. The squad leader had picked three men to go with them, and to Gyles's surprise, only one of them belonged to Second

Platoon. Gyles stepped closer and eyed the police officer and National Guardsman standing near the front of the vehicle. He had seen them both around the camp but didn't know them.

Weaver caught the sergeant's apprehensive stare and moved between him and the new guys. "How are you feeling, boss?"

"Like I lost a fight with truck."

Weaver looked him up and down and said, "You sure you're up for this?"

Gyles laughed. "Funny, that was the same question your mom asked me last time we were together."

"Fuck you," Weaver said.

"Yes, she did." He smiled.

"Yup, G-Man is back." Weaver laughed.

Gyles pointed to the two men. "Who we got here?"

Weaver turned toward the cop in a Vines City Police Department uniform. Like Luke, he wore a bulletproof vest, but it was smaller and not emblazoned with SWAT on the front. The man was mid-thirties with short hair and a square jaw. He carried a short-ened carbine with iron sights and a holstered Glock on his right hip. "This is Mike Sinclair. According to Luke, he knows the terrain better than anyone else around here, and he's local law. Can't hurt us—just in case we run into locals, ya know?"

Gyles nodded his agreement. "And this one?" he said, pointing to a skinny Private First Class with stubble on his face. After the attacks, Gyles didn't push grooming standards; they were in mixed company and had lost ninety percent of their men to a ravaged mob. Shaving sort of fell off the priority list.

"Private Aaron Mathews—same deal—he's hunted these woods; he knows the area."

Gyles looked up at the turret and recognized Corporal Jeremy Collier already positioned there. A big man, an overfed Nebraska boy who wouldn't look out of place on a Cornhusker defensive line, he was from Weaver's First Squad, one of their M240 machine gunners. But now, instead of the M240, he was holding an M4 that looked comically small in the big man's grip. "Where's your weapon, Corporal?"

Collier looked at Weaver, who answered for him. "Not worth taking it along. We have under three hundred 7.62 rounds for our remaining machine guns. Doesn't make sense to split the ammo. If we run into something, we can button up. Here, though, they might need it."

Pointing to the Humvee, Gyles said, "Well, you've covered the bases. Let's mount up and see what we can find."

They opened the doors and stuffed their gear inside before piling in. Officer Sinclair sat behind the wheel, with Mathews behind him while Gyles climbed into the front passenger seat, in front of Weaver.

Sinclair had the Hummer up and was navigating them down the road and into the tree-covered forest. "Where you are taking us today, Mike?" Gyles asked.

The man kept his eyes on the road and his hands on the wheel. "There is a small gas station and market at the edge of the forest. It doesn't have a name, and it's not on the map, but we've both been there."

Gyles leaned forward and twisted to look at the private behind him. "What's 'there'?"

Mathews raised his eyebrows as he thought. "It's like a little town," he said. "Market and some houses. Old man that runs the shop lives there. He makes good jerky."

"More details?" Gyles said.

"Jerky, yeah—like deer, turkey, beef—"

"No," Gyles interrupted. "What else is in the area? You ever been on a recon before, kid? Is there shit there were looking at?"

Laughing, Mike answered for the boy. "Well, there is a gas station," Mike added. "I don't know about diesel, but they have kerosene for sure."

Gyles turned his head and smiled. "That's smart thinking; the Hummers and Raps can run on Kerosene."

"They can?" Mathews asked.

"Yup, don't go telling the motor pool sergeant about it, but kero will get us where we need to go."

Mike slowed and made a turn off the narrow road they were on, maneuvering onto a wide, two-lane gravel road. The trees were far from the shoulder here, and the elevation of the road let them see far into the distance. Most of the horizon was a green line of forest but looking to the east, they could see the thin fingers of black smoke reaching up.

"Is there a town over there?" Gyles asked.

Mike turned his head and shook it no. "That's the interstate. Burning vehicles, most likely. There are some homes and farms that way too."

"Zoomies are bombing the shit out of them," Weaver said from the back. "You hear all the airstrikes last night?"

"There could be survivors out there," Gyles mumbled. "They are dropping bombs on survivors."

Weaver frowned. "It is what it is."

Gyles nodded and looked away, knowing his friend was right; there was nothing they could do about it. "It is what it is."

They held their thoughts the rest of the way down the road. Gyles kept his eyes to the window, watching the trees and signs that marked hiking trails or picnic areas pass by. Occasionally, he would look back to the horizon at the pillars of smoke and wonder what was at the bottom of them—were there battles raging beyond the trees? Were there people out there who needed help? Should he be trying to contact his command instead of hiding in the woods? He shook his head, unable to fight off the thoughts.

He grabbed at the SINCGARS military radio handset in the radio rack and powered it up. The vehicle also had an older version of Blue Force Tracker mounted in a steel rack, a system that uses GPS to track vehicles on a map in real time. He fumbled with the side buttons but couldn't power it on. Weaver leaned between the seats and shouted at him. "National Guard, brother, don't bother. That shit is ancient, and the radio doesn't even have the proper crypto. Don't even waste your time trying to hit civilian bands with that box."

Gyles sighed, frustrated, and tossed the handset back to the console. The vehicle slowed quickly, and Gyles put a hand on the dash to catch himself. He looked to Mike and then to the road ahead. In the center of the gravel path was a red pickup truck sitting motionless, the cab appearing empty. "Go ahead and stop us here," Gyles said. "Don't get any closer."

He leaned back in the seat and looked up. "What do you see, Collier?" he shouted to his man in the turret.

"Same as you, Sergeant. Pickup dead in the road. It's a Toyota, so nothing out of the ordinary."

"Okay, smartass—just keep scanning. You see anything, call out. We're going for a walk." He turned and looked at Weaver. "Let's have a closer look. Mike, you stay buttoned up. Regardless of what happens to us, you make it back to the camp. Mathews, you're going to unass and keep an eye on our six."

"What?" the kid said, his eyes getting big.

"Just make sure nothing sneaks up behind us," Gyles barked.

Mathews nodded and placed a hand on the door latch, waiting for the others to move. The team dismounted together with Gyles moving in a single motion, his barrel sweeping the space to the right of the vehicle then wrapping around the front and pointing at the pickup truck. He held, waiting for Weaver to move up to the front left of the Hummer and cover his blind spots.

Collier said in a bass-filled tone, "Got you covered." He tried speaking low but everything Collier said was at a shout. Normally a good trait for a machine gunner, but not at all appreciated today.

"Okay, we're moving," Gyles called out. He didn't turn to look at Weaver but could see in his peripheral that the man was making a same half-circle path, arcing out then back toward the truck. As Gyles moved closer, he could see that the back window of the pickup was missing, and there were gunshots in the driver's door.

"Battle damage on this side, boss," Weaver called out, not halting his movements.

"Same over here," Gyles said. He moved in and stopped just in front of the bumper on the right side. He rose up and aimed at the cab. Sidestepping, he moved around to the driver's door and quickly pulled back. A man was lying over the bench seat, the back of his white T-shirt red with coagulated blood. Gyles stepped back and leaned out to see into the bed of the truck. The inside held a pair of backpacks and what could have been a bundled-up tent, possibly a pair of sleeping bags. He flinched when he heard the passenger door creak open. Weaver pointed his barrel inside, moving the man's arm. He then reached in and pulled out a small handgun and placed it on the cab roof.

Weaver pointed at the console. "The ignition is on. Truck probably ran itself out of gas." He leaned in then pointed at the floor. "I'd say from the amount of stains on the carpet, this guy bled out. But who the hell shot him?" Both men backed away and spun out, searching the terrain again.

"You think the shooter is still here?" Gyles asked.

"All the gear is here so it wasn't a robbery, or not one that worked." Weaver scratched at his head. "I don't know, but we have to assume the infected aren't the only bad guys up ahead."

Gyles nodded his agreement. "Let's get this thing off the road." He moved back to the cab and leaned in, cranking the wheel and putting the truck in neutral. He then pointed to the HUMVEE and directed Mike forward. Moving slowly, the Hummer pushed the truck off the road, the body still inside.

"What about the gear?" Weaver asked.

Gyles shrugged. "We know where it's at—if we get that desperate on the return trip, we'll grab it. For now, let's leave it."

He moved around to the HUMVEE and climbed back inside, looking at Mike. "How far are we from this place you were talking about?"

"Just over the next rise."

Gyles scratched his head and ran his fingers through his hair. "The way that guy was heading, he must have come from there."

"Most likely," Weaver added from the back. "That hole in his back—it couldn't have been far."

Exhaling deeply, Gyles sighed. "Okay, stay alert. Let's see what's waiting for us."

CHAPTER FOURTEEN

DAY OF INFECTION PLUS TEN, 1130 HOURS

GW National Forest, Virginia.

I t wasn't a town by any standards. With just four aging structures scattered along a patch of road, Gyles wouldn't even consider it a community. Beyond it was an intersection where the gravel road they were traveling east on crossed a paved road that went north and south. There was no blinking light, not even a four-way stop sign.

At the intersection was a gas station on the southwest corner, across from it on the northeast side, a small gift shop. In the intersection was a vehicle collision, a mess of twisted still-smoking wreckage. The two vehicles had burned so it was impossible to tell who or what caused the mess, or even if there was anyone inside.

The men were stopped at the crest of a hill looking down at the buildings. The trees ended just behind them and turned to tall grass and pasture. They were leaving the edge of the national forest and moving onto a county road. "All right, Mike, bring us up nice and easy," Gyles said. "Mathews, I am starting to question your upbringing; how in the hell you going to call a pack of shacks a town?"

"I said it was kind of like a town," Mathews protested.

Mike let his foot off the brake and the vehicle rolled ahead, gravity pulling it down the hill. The diesel engine hummed at just above an idle. Gyles surveyed the four homes less than a hundred yards ahead of them. All of them were of similar construction, painted white with flat roofs. They were all in bad shape; it was hard to tell if anyone had lived in them at all.

Reading his mind, Mathews leaned forward. "The store owner lives in that place, there on the end. The big one." He pointed to the home furthest away on the left side of the road. "The rest aren't really houses. This place used to be one big farm, then the old man turned the other buildings in cabins that he would rent out to travelers. He stopped doing that a couple years ago."

Gyles thought of asking him why he stopped renting the cabins but realized he didn't care; his focus was on the gas station and its market ahead of them. The vehicle rolled past the buildings and stopped just short of the intersection, with the gas station quickly coming up on their right. There was a small blue sedan parked at one of the pumps. The front windshield was pockmarked from obvious gunfire—three impacts just above the steering wheel.

"I got a couple bodies over here, Sergeant. Your nine o'clock," Collier said from the turret, the echo from his loud voice causing Gyles to cringe.

Gyles turned to the left and could see the bare feet of a man lying in the grass. He sat up higher in the seat and saw the second body just beyond it. "Cut the engine," he said to Mike.

The rumbling of the diesel stopped and they sat in silence, listening. Gyles lifted his rifle and looked through the magnification of the optics, surveying the burnt-out vehicles. Even close, it was impossible to tell if anyone was in them. He opened the door and stepped onto the street. He waited, listening to the other men doing the same. His ears tuned into the surroundings for any sounds of activity, his eyes dialed in for movement; he was focused.

"You want me in the turret or out there, Sergeant —" Collier's voice boomed.

Gyles flinched, his jaw clenched. "What the fuck?" Gyles snapped back. "Seriously, bro? I know we are outside, but let's use this time to practice our inside voices."

"Aww... shit," he said just below a shout, a hand slapping over his mouth. He removed it and in a hoarse hurricane whisper said, "My bad, Sergeant. You know shooting the two-forty always gets me talking loud."

Tossing a thumbs up, Gyles nodded to him. "It's

fine, just stay with the vehicle... oh, and try not telling the entire county what we are doing."

Gyles leaned over the hood of the vehicle and signaled for the other two men to approach the bodies. Weaver moved toward them, walking heel-to-toe, rifle up. Mike stood back, his rifle aiming off to the left, covering the blind spots. It impressed Gyles that the lawman had tactical awareness. It didn't surprise him, but he was pleased nonetheless. Weaver looked down at the bodies and shook his head before moving back, keeping his rifle up toward the distant buildings.

He returned to the cluster of men near the Hummer. "Man and a woman. Both have been there at least overnight." Weaver stopped. "Fuck, they are just kids, man, and both are blistered with gunshots."

"Infected?" Gyles asked, already knowing it was a stupid question.

Shrugging, Weaver looked back toward the pair, his eyebrow raised. He then looked back to Gyles. "Hell if I know. Da fuck does an infected look like when they are dead?"

"Contact!" Collier bellowed from the turret. He was standing, leaning out with his rifle pointed toward the gas station. In the search of the bodies, Gyles had taken his eyes off his sector, and a man had wandered through an open doorway. He cursed himself for becoming distracted. Simple mistakes can get you killed on a patrol.

The man was stumbling forward, his abdomen

bloodied, his hands outstretched to the sides in a crucifix.

"Hold your fire! He's not armed," Gyles said, moving away from the vehicle, toward the bullet-scarred car at the gas pumps between him and the station's door. For the first time he noticed a slumped body in the driver's seat of the car lying over the center console. Dammit, he hadn't cleared it. Another mistake. He needed to slow down.

He stopped and made a visual search of the vehicle through the side window, seeing only the already bloating body. He turned and saw that Mathews wasn't moving, the young soldier still posted up at the back of the HUMVEE. "Move your ass, Private. Cover me," Gyles shouted as he repositioned at the hood of the sedan, keeping the engine block between him and the building.

The wounded man staggered ahead two more steps. He was trying to speak, but only shallow grunts left his mouth. The man's foot lifted then wavered, and he collapsed to a knee. Gyles rose, his rifle locked in on the man. He kept the red dot on the man's bloodied chest as he tried to search the empty windows of the station. Through the ACOG (Advanced Combat Optical Gunsight), with both eyes open, he could see blood-soaked gauze covering what appeared to be a bad gut wound. The man was old and gray-bearded, his face pale from blood loss.

Gyles looked left and right then called over his shoulder, "Cover the station windows; I'm moving up."

He passed between the gas pumps, keeping his head down and racing forward to the kneeling man. Just as he arrived, the man collapsed to the ground on his back. Looking for other wounds, Gyles ran a gloved hand down the arm closest to where he crouched. "Are you infected? Are you bit... scratched?"

"Infec...ted? Infected from what? I'm gutshot, boy," the old man said, trying to turn his head and failing.

The old man's lips were cracked and bloodied, and red foam had settled at the corners of his mouth. Gyles removed a bottle of water from a hip pocket, twisted off the top, and put it to the man's lips, allowing him to drink.

"You alone?"

The man strained and coughed, his voice garbled. "Yes. Ain't nobody here but me."

"What happened, buddy? Who shot you?" Gyles looked back and could see that the rest of his team was moving up, creating a bubble of security around him. Gyles relaxed his hold on the rifle, knowing he was covered, but kept his hand on the pistol grip.

The man tried to lift his head again before it collapsed back to the blacktop. "Lotta traffic," he whispered. "Too much traffic, so many people on the road day and night." The old man paused and took in several breaths, his eyes opening and closing. He looked up at Gyles. "They was young folks. They come in here just the other night." He tried to lift his head again. Gyles put a hand on the old man's shoulder. The man lifted his right hand and pointed to where the bodies lay on the far side of the road. "I think they're dead."

"Yeah." Gyles nodded and looked at the bare foot lying motionless in the grass. "We found 'em; nothing we can do for them."

"They were good kids. They come in here just after dark. Good kids," the man said again. "They filled up their truck, bought some supplies... water, food, stuff like that." The old man coughed again. "Lots of folks stop here before heading to the campgrounds, hard to pick out a campsite in the dark. They asked if it was okay if they rested in their truck until morning come."

Gyles searched the area, not seeing any truck. "Was it a red Toyota?"

The old man's eyes grew with recognition. "Yeah, how'd you know?"

"Found the driver dead a few miles up the road. You know how that happened?"

The man licked at his chapped lips. Gyles brought down the bottle and gave him another drink. "I done it. I shot him." He coughed violently; the bloody foam at the corners of his mouth grew. "At least I hope I done it; that son of a bitch killed those kids, and Susan, and whoever was in that other car in the road yonder," he said before closing his eyes tight. He opened them again and looked at Gyles.

He pointed at the intersection. "That feller came

in and did that, driving like a bat out of hell, he hit that car. The driver of the other car was killed, but that asshole walked away from it. He walked away with the other car burning like it was none of his business. Nothing for him to be concerned with.

"He run up in my station like he'd done nothing wrong, shouting at me. He demanded I give him a vehicle. I told him no, that I was going to call the police.

"I tried the phone but nothing. They didn't answer. The guy gets all agitated and pulls a pistol on me." The old man stopped to have another coughing fit. Gyles let him finish and used the corner of the man's shirt to wipe his chin.

The man took a labored breath and sighed. "He told me to give him my truck or he'd kill me." He looked at the bullet-pocked parked sedan. "Susan... from the gift shop... she'd locked up for the night and stopped to fill her tank. She was just in the wrong place at the wrong time. The man turned toward her, and she saw his gun. She screamed and ran back to her car. He shot me in the gut then ran after her. I heard the gunshots and those kids screaming." A tear rolled down the man's cheek.

"I keep a rifle behind the counter. I got to it, but he'd already shot Susan and those kids. He was in their truck trying to drive away. I pumped it full of rounds as he moved down the road." He shook his head. "I kept trying the phone, calling for help. Nobody come. I saw a few cars on the road; they all went right past that wreck, hardly slowing down. Like it wasn't even there."

Gyles turned to Mathews and called him forward. The private was quickly beside him. "Morgan," Mathews said in a faint voice, kneeling to put a hand on the man's shoulder. The man looked up at him with recognition. He forced a smile but didn't speak.

"Mathews, I need you stay with him while we clear the buildings."

The private nodded, not taking his eyes off the old man. His hand had moved from the old man's shoulder and was now gripping his bloody palm. Weaver and Mike had moved forward and were fanning out. Gyles got to his feet and joined them at the front of the station. Feet away from the door, he could see inside. The shelves were still fully stocked and untouched, the lights out. He moved to the glass door and looked inside. Weaver reached out and, waiting for a nod from Gyles, pulled it open.

The inside of the store was damp and musty with the power out. Gyles could see smeared blood on the white tile floor. He moved inside, walking to the counter and looking over it, seeing more blood on the far side. Moving back along the floor, looking down aisles, he saw the blood trail led to an area of first aid supplies. Strips of gauze and bandages were dumped out. Several first aid kits were opened and scattered. A Ruger Mini-14 lay on the floor with an empty magazine box next to it.

After a quick lap through the store, Gyles found the place as empty as the old man said it was. He moved to a back-corner area filled with automotive supplies, finding a half dozen red five-gallon plastic gas cans. He pointed at them and told Weaver to get to work on filling them with diesel if they had it. He saw another shelf on the back wall with sealed single-gallon cans of kerosene. There were less than ten of them; it wouldn't make much of a difference. He moved through the store and to a back door. Holding the handle, he waited and listened intently before opening it.

He found something outside that would be even more useful to them—a Ford pickup truck with a land-scaping trailer attached to it. On the trailer was a strapped-down riding lawnmower, a pair of push mowers, and some weed edgers. Gyles looked back, seeing that Mike was just behind him. He pointed at the truck and trailer. "Get Collier and get this thing stripped down, get all that junk off the trailer. We can use the truck and trailer to get as much out of here and back to the camp as possible."

Mike nodded and turned away to get Collier. Gyles let the door close then moved back to the front of the store and knelt by the old man, whose eyes were now shut. Mathews had the old man's head propped up on a folded blanket. Gyles looked at the blanket and asked Mathews, "Where'd you get that?"

Mathews pointed to a set of picnic tables at the end of the gas station. Gyles had seen it before but didn't pay much attention to it. The young man lifted something up and showed it to Gyles. "There was this too," he said.

Gyles took it in his hand. It was an MRE wrapper. He examined it and looked back at Mathews. "You found this over there?" he asked.

"Yeah, looks like the kids might'a been eating MREs when the shooting started. Stuff is opened and dumped out, like they never really got into it." Mathews looked back at the table and to Gyles. "Sergeant, where you think they got MREs?"

Gyles bit at his lower lip, holding the brown package wrapper. He turned it in his hand. "Lots of people have them, I guess, especially campers."

"No," the old man coughed.

Gyles looked down at him. The man's eyes were still closed but his lip was quivering. "They said there is a roadblock about five miles north. Military is stopping all northbound traffic, giving out those food pouches and water to folks that need it. But not letting anyone get back on 81 to go north."

"They told you this?" Gyles asked.

"Yes." The old man wheezed then relaxed again. "'Cause of the riots, they said. Police won't let anyone north." He opened his eyes and looked at Gyles. "When I saw your army truck, I thought that was where you came from."

Looking over the old man, he watched as Weaver pushed a shopping cart filled with the empty plastic gas cans toward the pumps. The bottom of the cart was stacked with the cans of kerosene. He stopped by Gyles and looked down at the old man, shaking his head slowly side to side. "Found the pump controls and lit it up."

"You all taking my fuel?" the old man said.

"We'll write you an IOU," Gyles said, squeezing his shoulder. "We'll pay for anything we take."

The man smiled. Gyles winced, seeing the blood on his teeth. "Take what you need. Power is out, but it auto switched to a low-pressure pump. It runs on batteries on the roof. Take what you can while we got juice to pump it," the old man whispered.

Gyles looked at the three rows of pumps, taking note of the yellow handle at one on the end. Weaver saw what he was looking at and nodded. "I'll get the cans topped off and fill the Hummer."

As he spoke, the Ford pickup with the long trailer attached rolled around the corner. Mike had off-loaded all lawnmowing equipment and dumped things that had been stuck in the truck bed. Gyles looked across at Mathews and said, "Get your friend comfortable in the back of the truck and help Mike get as much loaded as you can. Anything left you can come back for later, okay?"

The injured man spoke up. "Nope. Just get me home to my place. I'll be okay there," he whispered. "I ain't leaving here."

Gyles looked down at him; there was no doubt in any of their minds that the old man wasn't going to make it. Even in the best of circumstances, being gutshot wasn't survivable without a proper trauma center. "I'll make sure they get you home," Gyles said.

The old man opened his eyes. "And I'll need that IOU for anything you boys take. I know my inventory too, so make sure it's all listed. Don't test me, son."

Mathews squeezed the old man's palm. "I'll make sure it's all written down, Mister Morgan."

CHAPTER FIFTEEN

GW National Forest, Morgan's Corner Store, Virginia.

I t took them the better part of two hours to load the truck and trailer with all the food, water, and diesel fuel it could hold. Gyles made sure that Mike and Mathews delivered the man to his home, along with a detailed list of what they had taken. If the man had family, they wanted to make sure the government paid its debt. While they delivered Morgan to his home, the rest of them finished loading the supplies and ensuring everything was tied down.

Gyles carefully walked around the front of the Humvee, where Weaver was opening a new can of tobacco. He had a log of the chewing tobacco sitting on the hood of the vehicle. Weaver looked back toward Collier, who was standing near the Ford pickup, loading cases of water. "Can you believe this? With all the killing going on, and this man found a way to kill even more," he said. "What the hell was he thinking?"

Gyles stared at the wreckage in the road. "He was running away from something, and we both know what. The infected have got to be close."

"What are you looking to do?" Weaver asked. "You want to go find them?"

"No, I don't want to find them," Gyles said, shaking his head. "I'm going to send M and M back to camp with the truck and the trailer; that's the priority." Gyles had not taken his eyes off the wrecked cars. "I'll have them let Luke know about the supplies here and everything we got. If he's smart, he'll send a team for everything else, get it all moved back to camp."

"We're not going then?" Weaver said. "We're not going back?"

"Can't," Gyles said. "That old man said there could be a checkpoint up ahead. We need to move on up the road and see if we can find this military roadblock."

Weaver turned his head and spit a wad of tobacco. "You think they are still there, boss?"

Gyles shook his head then heard footfalls behind him. Turning, he saw Mike and Mathews returning from Morgan's house. Both men were holding their rifles loosely to their front, their heads hanging. They walked past the pumps and stood between the Ford and the Humvee. Collier finished with a tie-down and stepped back.

Gyles looked to Mike. "How is he?"

The officer sighed and shook his head. "He's gone." He held out a brown leather hygiene bag. "The old man had a virtual pharmacy in his bathroom, everything from some pretty high-strength pain killers to antibiotics. Figured we could use them. You want me to take this stuff back to that doctor?"

Gyles took the bag and looked at the bottles, considering his answer. He still didn't have much trust or faith in Doctor Howard. He decided he would hold onto them until he could talk it over with his medic, Corporal Rodriguez. "This is good, Mike. I think I'll hold them for now and talk it over with the Doc when I get back."

"When will that be?" Mike asked.

Gyles hesitated to look out at the road then to the truck being loaded with supplies. "Listen, I want you to head back with Mathews, tell Luke what we have here, and let him know we are continuing on with the recon. We'll try and be back before sundown."

Mike raised his eyebrows. "You sure? This stuff isn't going anywhere. Maybe we can all move out together and just grab this on the way back."

Frowning, Gyles said, "No, food and water is too important to risk, and they need fuel or they won't be able to bug out if..."

"If," Mike said, knowing exactly what Gyles meant. "But, if it's so important to get this stuff back to camp, then come with us. We have food now; we can hold out, let help come to us."

Not used to being questioned, Gyles put his hands

on his hips and exhaled. He was ready to improve his argument when Weaver intervened. "Mike, you take care of the people, and we'll take care of Army stuff. That cool?" Weaver said.

Mike nodded, knowing he was in a losing argument. "Understood. You guys just be careful and make sure you get back to the camp." He walked toward the two men and extended his hand. "I'll make sure Luke gets a full rundown on what's going on. You ain't back by dark, we're going to come looking for you."

Gyles rubbed his chin and smiled. "At least give us two days. I'm not looking to spend the night out here, but Murphy, ya know," he said, returning the handshake.

"Yeah, I know," Mike said, turning to the truck and mounting up.

Gyles stood by and watched the truck pull out and head back up the road toward the camp, the trailer completely overloaded with cases of food and water. He looked back to their own vehicle. It was just as well-supplied, with enough food to last three days, if you count snack cakes and Slim Jims as food. The back rack of the Hummer held 4 five-gallon cans of diesel on a rack, and the tank was completely topped off.

He looked at the two men beside him and told them it was time to go. Collier headed for the turret and Gyles shook him off. "Just stay inside for now. We'll go buttoned up from here on out. We don't fight unless we have to."

Collier nodded, seeming relieved at the idea. He

moved around to the back passenger door. "Oh no, Corporal; no laid-back day of window licking for you," Weaver said, pointing to the driver's seat.

Collier pursed his lips and nodded. "I got you. Makes no difference to me because I like driving anyway," he bellowed, trying to hold back a laugh.

"Well, try liking it with your inside voice, Mister Megaphone," Gyles said, holding a finger to his lips.

"Damn, boss, did you just give Corporal Collier here a nickname? Fucking Mega, Mister Megaphone." Weaver laughed.

The comment busted the dam, and Collier let loose with a laugh that could have been heard back at the camp. Gyles shook his head and shoved the big man toward the Hummer, telling them to mount up. They'd all been balling up stress for the last few days, and it felt good to laugh about something, even if it was about how big a buffoon Collier was. "Okay, Mega, kick the tires and light the fires," he said. "Let's get some distance on this place."

Mega's booming laugh was still bouncing around the armored cab of the Humvee as they made the turn onto the highway and headed east. The terrain and scenery quickly changed. It was like moving across borders in some old movie, from color into black and white. The road went from dirt to pavement. Less than a mile onto the paved road, they made the turn onto the interstate ramp headed north.

Gyles spun his head, looking for landmarks and writing a mile marker number into his notebook.

"Make sure we can find our way back, boys," he said, the others nodding.

They were on the interstate now. It was crowded and backed up with abandoned vehicles. And there was something else; they were surrounded by death. As Mega slowed to run on the shoulder of the road along a line of stalled vehicles, Gyles could see that the cars, in fact, hadn't been abandoned. They were covered with gore, hand marks left by the doomed occupants, windshields streaked with blood. Gyles clenched his hands, instinctively checking the location of his rifle.

"What the hell happened here?" Weaver mumbled.

Gyles didn't want to say it; they already knew what had happened. Mega moved the vehicle across the lanes and into the grass-covered center of the median as the shoulder became too congested. They came over a slight rise and it all changed again. The cars became smoldering shells of what they once were. The men immediately recognized the destruction left by airstrikes. They'd spent enough time in Iraq and Afghanistan to know the death blows of heavy ordnance.

"Getting thick up here, boss," Mega said in his typical loud voice. "If it gets any worse we'll need a new route."

It woke Gyles's nerves, causing him to stiffen and sit higher in his seat. The driver was right; he could see that the wreckage was spanning out like a blooming flower, but somehow it was thinner right down the middle. Gyles pointed to a clear route, and Mega weaved the vehicle through the mess of destroyed cars. They drove through a large crater, the Humvee rocking side to side, the vehicle's suspension protesting as it moved over crushed concrete.

Gyles suddenly knew why there were less cars in the center of the road—this was ground zero for a volley of bombs. The Air Force must have pounded the area, turning it into a mass of craters. They indiscriminately killed everything. The people here were fleeing, yet the military had bombed them on the road. Gyles spun his head back to Weaver; he could tell from his friend's wide eyes that he'd come to the same conclusion.

Mega stopped the Humvee, and Gyles turned back to the front. "What is it?"

"I think I see something," the driver said. "Something alive."

CHAPTER SIXTEEN

DAY OF INFECTION PLUS TEN, 1540 HOURS

Interstate 81, Virginia.

Ahead of them, in the destruction of the road, Gyles thought he spotted a flash of movement. He strained his eyes and lifted his binoculars, seeing only the smoldering vehicles and bombed out craters left by the Air Force. He shook his head and looked back at Weaver, who was scanning from a side window. "You see anything?"

"Nothing from back here," Weaver said, his eyes going from window to window. "Mega, you sure you saw something? What was it?"

Mega leaned his head over the wheel, straining. "It was a man; he was waving at us." He pointed toward a spot where a highway overpass had once been. Now it was a pile of rubble with a narrow path going through it. "He was right up there."

"You're positive it wasn't an infected?" Gyles asked.

Mega squinted his eyes and frowned. "Well, about as possible as anything. How can I be sure of that?"

Gyles turned back again toward Weaver. "What do you think?"

Weaver looked in the direction Mega had pointed. He seemed to ponder the question before saying, "Well, nobody is there now. It's on our way, so let's have us a closer look."

Gyles pointed his finger, and Mega put the Hummer back into drive, slowly rolling them ahead. On hyper-alert now, Gyles kept his eyes glued to the shoulder of the road on the right side as Weaver scanned the inbound side of the vehicle. They approached the narrow path through what used to be the highway overpass. Large blocks of broken concrete were pushed and scrapped aside, making a lane just wide enough for the Humvee.

"Looks like someone with a big dozer or plow truck busted a path back open after the Air Force closed it," Mega said. "You just can't stop a good ol' boy from moving. If they want to go somewhere, they are going to go. Fuck the war. You know what I'm saying?"

"What the hell are you talking about, Mega?" Weaver exclaimed from the back. "Nobody knows what you are saying."

"Sure, you do. I mean all this bombing to try and keep folks off the road. Keep them from moving. Yeah... maybe it is to stop the spread of infection. But people

like me... folks like me, we won't care about that."
Mega's white knuckles still gripped the wheel. "Oh
yeah, you can tell folks, 'Stay home, lock your doors,
don't go outside.' But to me and mine, that's all noise. If
I wasn't with you all in this uniform, nothing would be
able to stop me from getting back to my folks in
Lincoln."

"Lincoln, Nebraska?" Weaver laughed. "What is
that, like fifteen hundred miles?"

Mega nodded his head. "Doesn't matter, I'd walk
the entire thing with a heavy pack on my back to get
home. Family is important."

"Stop," Gyles said, raising a hand.

The vehicle halted just past the break in the overpass. On the right-hand side of the road a man stood
staring at them. He wore red-checkered flannel and
blue jeans, a green John Deere cap on his head. The
man wasn't waving, and he had no expression on his
face. He just stood there motionless. Gyles searched
the terrain and could see that just behind the man was
a well-beaten and rusted pickup truck. It had the words
Carson Family Farms on the driver's door.

The trio in the vehicle looked at the man, waiting
for a response that didn't come. "That what you saw,
Mega?" Gyles said without moving his head.

"Yeah, pretty sure that's him. But he was waving
earlier," Mega said in a loud whisper that would have
made Gyles laugh under other circumstances.

The platoon sergeant exhaled and gripped his rifle.
"Weaver, stand ready to get up in that turret and cover

me when I step out. This could be an ambush to steal our truck and gear. If it turns dirty, lock me out and no matter what, you don't give up the vehicle or your-selves. You got it?"

From the back seat, Weaver hesitated to speak.

"Sergeant Weaver, do you understand?" Gyles said again.

Weaver sighed. "You do what you got to do, and so will we."

Gyles grinned, knowing that was about the best response he would get from his friend. He put his hand to the combat lock and popped the passenger door. As it clunked open, the man outside flinched. "Well, that's a good sign," he said in a faint voice to himself. "Scared of me is better than mad at me."

He heard the clanking of the vehicle's hatch and knew that Weaver would be up behind him and scan-ning from his high commanding position. From the turret, he would be able to see more than Gyles could on the ground. He pulled his rifle up to his chest and stepped away from the Humvee, pressing the door closed behind him. His eyes scanned the terrain to his front and behind the red-flannelled man. The farm truck was empty. The woods and field beyond the highway were motionless except for the swaying vegetation.

Gyles focused his eyes on the civilian. "What are you doing out here?"

The man looked at him and then toward the road. "Sorry, I thought maybe you were someone else," the man said, looking away, like he might want to run. "You can just continue on."

"Someone else? Who exactly were you expecting to see?"

The man looked up and locked eyes with Gyles. "Someone that could help."

"And we can't?" Gyles asked.

The man raised a hand and waved it toward the death and destruction on the highway. "You all did this. You killed all these people." The man scowled. "Yeah, I'm sure you aren't in the helping business."

Gyles suddenly felt ashamed; he hadn't even considered that fact. It was his people, the military, who had done most of this. Not the infected. His shoulders slacked and his weapon dropped lower in his grip. "Listen, I don't know what happened here. My unit is separated from our command. We have civilians and local law enforcement holed up in a camp not far from here, if you need help—"

"No," the man said. "We aren't going anywhere. We need a doctor, not a place to stay."

"You have wounded?" Gyles said. "I have a doctor back at my camp."

The man shook his head and looked around. "No— we aren't leaving the farm. My son is injured, the wife sent me to try and find some antibiotics for him. Medicine."

Gyles thought about the leather bag of drugs Mike had given him. He looked back at Weaver and to the man. "We have some medicine; maybe we can help."

The man took a step back, looking at his truck then back to the soldiers. He nodded his head and said, "Okay, you all follow me." With no other response, he turned and moved back to his truck.

Gyles held his own position for a moment longer and scanned the area. Beyond the truck he saw a trail and a place where the wire fence along the highway had been cut. It was how the man had gotten so close to the highway.

Gyles turned and entered the Humvee. When he looked back, the big farm truck was already moving. He said to Mega, "Follow him."

"Where we are going?" Mega asked.

Gyles shook off the question. "I don't know, but the man needs help, so for now we'll do what we can."

Mega smiled. "Fair enough, boss." He pulled the Humvee off to the grassy shoulder to follow the farm truck.

When Gyles looked back, he could see that Weaver had remained up in the turret. It was an advantageous position to be in now that they were covering another vehicle, and if the man was dirty and leading them into an ambush, Weaver's eyes and rifle in the turret could give them an advantage.

The farm truck passed through the tree line then skirted a field of soybeans before finding a narrow two-trek road. The truck kicked up a fine dust as it bounced over the terrain, and the Humvee followed close behind. They were moving away from the highway through fields of green that stretched to the horizon. There was no movement at all; it was the definition of isolation. The truck turned again and crossed over an old wooden bridge that spanned a narrow stream.

After traveling another five minutes, Gyles saw tall red barns and a white farmhouse on the horizon. Looking far off to the north, he could just see the makings of a blacktop road. The farm truck slowed and moved aside a square pole barn that looked recently built. The man shut off the truck and exited. He removed his green cap and wiped sweat from his forehead. Gyles reached behind him and grabbed the leather shaving bag filled with pills.

As Gyles went to order his men to stay alert, a door on the back of the steel building opened and two small children, a boy and a girl, ran out to hug the man. "Well shit," Gyles said.

He looked back at his soldiers. "Let's go. Weapons slung, okay?"

Gyles unlatched the door and stepped out. The man turned, the children looking up at the soldiers with wide eyes. Gyles smiled at them and stepped closer. "My name is Robert," he said to a blonde girl in a pink sundress who was maybe six years old.

She smiled back at him and clutched the farmer's leg. The man extended a hand to Gyles. "Name's Wayne Carson. These are my children. This one is Jenny and the other guy there is Tyler."

Gyles smiled, returning the handshake. He turned back to the other soldiers. "These are my friends." He pointed first to Weaver then to Collier. "That's Eric, and we call that big one right there Mega.

The young boy looked at the large soldier with curious eyes. "Like Megatron." The boy smiled. "Is he a robot?"

Mega puffed out his chest, grinning.

Weaver shook his head. "No—like megaphone because he is really loud and doesn't know how to whisper."

The children laughed, looking back at Mega, who had lost his grin. Gyles turned back to Wayne, holding open the bag. We have a few things that might help. Where are your wounded?"

Wayne looked back to the kids. "Jenny, take Tyler back to Nana and Grandpa. I'm going to go check on Mom and Steven, okay?"

The girl nodded and returned to the steel pole building. When they were back inside and Wayne heard the lock clunk shut, he pointed to the farm house and began walking toward it. "I put them all up in the steel building after those things managed to get into the house. The pole barn has no windows, steel walls, and access to the storm shelter."

Gyles nodded. He looked ahead at the old farm-house they were moving toward, and he could see that near the back porch, several bodies were stacked up. Wayne caught his stare and said, "I'll bury them later. Just been busy." He pointed to the farm. "They came just after noon. Killed my dogs and broke in the back windows. My oldest boy, Steven, was able to fight them back until I could get to my rifle. I don't know what they are, but the only thing they understand is bullets."

Gyles nodded. "We've had our own run-ins with them."

They passed the piled bodies and moved up old wooden steps onto the covered front porch. Gyles could see windows were broken and the back door had been smashed open. Wayne continued inside through an old screen door. Gyles stopped short of the doorway and looked at Mega. "Stand watch out here, okay? We don't need anything sneaking up on us."

The big man nodded and walked the porch, dropping into an old wooden rocking chair. Gyles was going to scold him for it but decided it wasn't worth the effort. He turned and stepped into the farmhouse with Weaver on his tail. They moved into a long hallway with tall ceilings and hardwood floors. They could hear muffled voices from a room ahead, and they moved in that direction. Turning a corner into a large dining room, Gyles froze.

Every window in the room had been broken. The walls were pocked with bullet holes, furniture broken and kicked over, family pictures lay on the floor in broken frames. In the center of the room was an old family dining table. Laid out across the table was a young boy. He couldn't have been older than sixteen. A dark-haired woman held a rag to his head and was swabbing his face. Gyles moved closer and could see that both the boy's arms were bandaged. An IV bag was hanging from an overhead light and running into the boy's upper arm. Dark-blue and purple streaks stretched from the wounds, up his arms, to his shoulders and neck.

Gyles stepped closer. "How long since he was—"

"Bit?" the woman said. "That's what those things did; they bit him."

Wayne stepped beside his wife and put a hand on her shoulder. "It's been about four hours. And he's been getting nothing but worse. He lost consciousness a couple hours after the attack." He looked at the woman. "Lori is a veterinarian. She's been doing the best she can for him."

"I'm not a vet; I just help at the clinic on weekends," she said, correcting her husband.

Gyles moved closer and, opening the bag, showed her the contents. She looked down at the unconscious boy on the table before turning back to Wayne. She shook her head. "We can't waste these soldiers' medicine. There is no coming back from this."

"Please, Lori, we've got to try," Wayne said.

A tear fell down Lori's cheek. "He's gone, Wayne." The woman looked back to the soldiers. "Everything they are saying, there is no cure for him. If something ain't done soon, he's going to wake up like those things out in the yard."

Wayne shook his head harshly and walked away. She turned back to Gyles, who looked at the corner of the table, where a stainless steel tray sat, holding a syringe and several glass vials. "I want him to get better as much as anyone, but he just keeps getting worse. I talked to the doctor—Doctor Meyers—who runs our clinic, and he said it's not going to happen. That when Steven wakes up he will be a monster."

"Meyer isn't a doctor; he's a veterinarian," Wayne said, raising his voice.

Gyles looked at her. "When did you talk to this doctor?"

"We have a CB radio in the back of the house. I talked to him a couple hours ago, but the radio went dead shortly after."

"How does he know so much about it?" Gyles asked.

The woman's face hardened. "Because he has been out dealing with it for the last three days," she said with a scowl.

Gyles put up his hands in surrender. He looked back at Weaver, who was slowly shaking his head from side to side. He faced the woman again. "Listen, ma'am, what can I do to help you? I have a doctor back at my camp; he's an expert with this stuff. But like your friend has told you—"

"There isn't a cure," she said.

Gyles frowned. "No, there isn't."

Wayne turned back from the wall and moved closer, stopping and standing behind his wife. His face was twisted in grief. He spoke with his voice breaking. "There's got to be something else we can do."

Lori turned and hugged the man. Both sobbed. Gyles took a step back; he wanted nothing more than to be a thousand miles away from the room. He'd rather be fighting the infected than standing there watching a family grieve for their son. Wayne let go of his wife and wiped his eyes before putting a hand on the boy's head. He looked up at Lori, then at Gyles, then at the steel tray. "If it's got to be done, I don't want her doing it."

Gyles wanted to refuse and walk out of the farmhouse, to get in the Humvee and return to camp. But looking at the broken faces of the parents in front of him, he knew that he couldn't. He nodded his head and stepped closer to the table. Wayne moved away to a wooden chair and sat heavily. He put his head in his hands and sobbed. Lori walked around the table and took the syringe. She picked up a glass vial and, using the syringe, pulled out all the liquid. Then she placed the full syringe on the tray.

Looking back to Gyles, she pointed at the syringe. "Just put the needle into the port on the IV line," she said, then moved to stand behind the farmer, putting her hands on his shoulders.

Gyles looked to Weaver, and Weaver stepped forward. "I'll do it."

Shaking his head, no, Gyles took the needle and held it, looking down at the boy on the table. He exhaled and held the line in his left hand. He bit down hard on his lower lip and slowly inserted the needle. His hands shaking, he pressed the plunger slowly until all the fluid was expended. He could hear the parents sobbing. Gyles removed the needle from the tube, snatched the leather bag, and turned to leave the room. He walked swiftly back onto the covered porch.

Mega quickly moved back to his feet. He looked at Gyles holding the brown leather bag. "You able to help them, Sergeant?"

Unable to speak, Gyles shook his head no.

The screen door closed behind them, and Gyles turned to see Weaver on the porch. "Can we get the hell out of here?"

Gyles nodded, and they started moving back toward their Humvee when an old man in faded blue coveralls stepped from the back door of the pole building. He was holding an old lever-action .30-30 in his hands. He looked to them and back at the house. "How is my grandson?"

Frowning, Gyles shook his head.

"I see," the old man said. "Where you boys off to?"

Gyles exhaled. "We were told the military had set up a roadblock on the highway. We were trying to find it when we bumped into Wayne."

The old man squinted and turned to the driveway, pointing with the end of the rifle. "Follow the drive and take a left. Just past the grain silos you'll see a gravel cut. Take that to the interstate and you'll see where the Army set up its little roadblock." The man looked back at Gyles and put a free hand to his chin. "I wouldn't go there if I were you."

"Why is that?"

"There was fighting over that way all night. Lots of bombs, machine guns. All sorts of things. The rumbling came at us until well after sunup. That fight is probably what pushed them crazy people toward our farm this afternoon. If I were you, I'd go the opposite direction from all of that."

Gyles nodded his understanding. "I see." He took a step toward the Humvee. "What are you all planning to do out here?" he asked.

The old man grimaced. "We're set up okay." He shook his head. "We should have moved to the cellar days ago. If we had... Steven would still be okay. We have canned goods, well water, everything we need in there. We first started hearing about those crazy attacks last week on the news. My wife and I have a small place in town, our retirement spot we moved to after I gave Wayne the farm. As things got nuttier on the news, we loaded up and came back here. We've been watching the news and the traffic. Was probably about four days ago when it got bad, and we started hearing the gun shots.

"But still nothing came out to the farm. We are located quite a hitch from town, and even if you are looking for it, you'll miss the turnoff from the highway. It was just pure bad luck, I reckon, that those crazy people found their way to the farm this afternoon. Maybe it was the dogs barking. I don't rightly know."

"So, you don't plan to leave then?" Gyles asked.

The old man pulled his rifle in. "You ain't looking to make us, are you?"

Gyles smiled. "No sir; you are far better off than

anything I'd have to offer you. We'll be on our way and wish you good luck."

The old man nodded. "Listen, if you go checking out the Army outpost, don't you come back this way. We don't need any more of them things following you here. And please don't tell anyone about us. We're hidden. I'd like it to stay that way."

"Can do," Gyles said. He pointed to the Humvee, and the men mounted back up. With the doors closed, Mega put them back on the gravel drive headed toward the military outpost.

CHAPTER SEVENTEEN

DAY OF INFECTION PLUS TEN, 1700 HOURS

Interstate 81, Virginia.

"Take us in slow," Gyles said.

On a high incline looking down, they already knew the military encampment was abandoned. Bypassing it wasn't an option; it was the reason they were here, and they had to search it. They needed information and supplies. Directly ahead, covering both sides of the interstate and the median, the path was blocked by a long strand of wire and interspersed with military and civilian law enforcement vehicles. It was a barricade, a wall that attempted to stop the flow of traffic but must have quickly been turned into a defensive perimeter as things on the ground went sideways.

Gyles reflected on his own experiences at the lab and at the armory and cringed at the thought of what the troops here must have gone through. "Get us close and kill the engine," Gyles said, surprised to find himself whispering.

Orange plastic barrels and concrete barriers funneled vehicle traffic from both the north and south lanes of the interstate into a single line that weaved onto the median. The once grass-covered field was now squared off by sandbag bunkers. A Stryker vehicle overlooking the entrance sat silently with a top hatch open. Like the rest of the bodies they'd seen since entering the interstate, the ones here were scattered on the ground in twisted poses. Gyles reached into a chest pocket and removed a shemagh that he wrapped around his face to cover the stench of death and decay that hung heavy in the air. Mega eased the truck up alongside the line of vehicles less than fifty meters from the makeshift gate and cut the engine.

They could see through the barricade; the path ahead was surprisingly clear for at least a hundred yards. Whatever had been holding this position was gone. Their vehicles and fighting positions overrun, the only thing left to let a traveler know that this position was once held, were bodies and spent brass casings on the ground.

The men sat still, holding their breath, heads not moving but eyes scanning the ghostly terrain around them. Every hair on the back of Gyles's neck was up, and he could hear the heavy breathing from the rest of his crew. None of the trio was new to war, but this was something entirely different to them.

"This is bad," Weaver whispered. "You sure about this?"

"It don't mean nothing," Mega answered, his voice cracking, his oversized hand squeezing the steering wheel. "It don't mean nothing."

They were looking directly into a kill zone. The pathway ahead was open; a narrowly constructed lift gate that once closed it was knocked from its stand. The sides of the lane had been blocked by hastily erected HESCO barriers—large fabric bags filled with stone to create walls—and sandbag berms. Along the face of the wall were strands of concertina wire now intertangled with bloated bodies. Soldiers dressed in ACUs still lay where they died, sprawled across the tops of barriers. Along the top of the wall places were cut out where mounted weapons nests once sat. A few of the big guns were still there, the barrels aimed up into the sky. Weaver leaned forward and pointed a hand at a body twitching in the wire ahead of them. The thing was wrenched into an unhuman pose halfway up the wall, its arm knocking into the wire.

"I see it," Gyles whispered.

"You think it's one of us—or one of them?" Mega asked, his head fixed straight ahead.

"If it's one of us, then why is it on the wrong side of the barrier caught up in that wire?" Weaver said.

"Well," Mega shrugged, "technically, we are on the wrong side of the barrier."

"You want to climb up there and find out?" Gyles

said. "Maybe ask him what team he is on, find out what his favorite color is?"

Mega's head turned to Gyles, his eyebrows raised. "Yeah, it's one of theirs, definitely."

"Thought so," Gyles said. Instinctively, his hand passed over the front of his vest, checking his magazine pouches and his sidearm. He then lifted his M4 and press-checked the magazine. "We're going out there. We're going to have a quick sweep, look for handheld radios, ammo, and weapons. Anything comes at us, we get back to the truck and button up, get the hell out of here," he said in a monotone voice that left no room for discussion. "Mega, dial down your volume control to its lowest setting. Actually, just hit mute on that boom box."

Without another word, Gyles put his hand on the latch and slowly pulled until it engaged, then eased the squeaking door open just enough that he could exit. He raised his rifle to the low ready, took three steps out from the Humvee, and took a knee. They'd done drills like this plenty of times, and the movements were second nature to him now. He could hear the light tapping of boot heels on the pavement and knew the other men were doing the same. In his head, Gyles counted to thirty and then stood, his head sweeping the surroundings. Nothing had changed.

The visual and aromatic feedback made him shudder. In the near proximity of death, his heart was racing from the surge of adrenaline. He knew if he let go of the rifle's pistol grip, his hand would be shaking like a leaf. He debated returning to the safety of the armored vehicle, locking up, and returning to the camp. As he choked back bile, he knew it was probably the smart thing to do, and nobody would question him for it. Nobody but himself. He came for a reason, and they had to press on. They needed ammo and answers.

Gyles clenched his jaw. *Fuck it, we are here to work, and that's what we are going to do.* He lifted his leg and stepped forward. Conscious of every footfall, he focused on stealth as he moved toward the break in the wall. His eyes were drawn toward the twitching creature in the wire. His mouth had gone dry, every breath a challenge to hold in. He resisted the impulse to vomit when he got a closer look at the entangled man.

The former human's neck was broken. He must have been partially paralyzed; the thing's eyes followed them, its only mobile arm slapping the wire in a constant drum beat. The *thwap, thwap, thwap* against the concertina wire, every motion, sent a tremble down Gyles's back. He wanted nothing more than to run a kill shot through the thing's skull. But they had to remain silent. He swiveled and could see his men patrolling behind him in a single column, Mega in the middle, Weaver taking rear security. Both men's eyes locked on the grotesque twitching creature.

Gyles looked at them and pointed two fingers at his eyes. Weaver swallowed hard and gave a knowing nod, turning back around to cover their rear.

Moving forward, Gyles found that the gateway was surprisingly clear of bodies. Just inside the perimeter, things weren't as tidy. The dead were stacked up, and they ringed around fighting positions. Bodies were in clusters where individual battles took place against men in life-or-death struggles. Gyles's own battle at the Vineyard Armory flashed to the forefront of his mind, and he froze, staring at the destruction of riddled bodies and scattered equipment. He swallowed hard, trying to get his mind back into the present, when he heard a low whistle from behind him. A light wisp, like a whip of wind. He turned and saw Mega pointing at something.

He wanted to be angry at the man for breaking noise discipline, but he was grateful for the distraction. He squinted, following what the soldier was pointing at. On the wall in one of the fighting positions, part of the sand bag barrier had tumbled away. Mangled corpses hung out of the wire over the wall. A uniformed man lay dead at the base of the wall. Gyles focused and half smiled; just to the right of the man was an MK19 lying on its side with the tripod legs in the air, an ammo can still partially attached. His eyes drifted to the right, where he could see the wooden crates of an ammo cache. There was ammo here, and by the looks of the boxes, a lot of it.

Gyles took a knee and let the men crowd in around him. He pointed to the 40-millimeter, belt-fed, automatic grenade launcher and looked at Mega. "Can we get that on the turret?" he whispered. He kept his finger pointed at the man, not allowing him to speak. "A nod yes or no will do."

Mega grimaced and dipped his chin.

"Okay, you two recover that weapon then. Don't dick around—just pack it up and get it in the truck; we can mount it later. Get back here and secure all of that ammo." He exhaled, taking another pass with his eyes. He'd seen no movement and, surrounded by the walls, he felt isolated from the outside. There could be hundreds of them beyond the HESCO barrier walls but, inside, they were alone. Even surrounded by the death, he almost felt secure. "I'll cover you while you work."

Weaver flashed a thumbs up and, with Mega, stepped off toward the dead trooper and the MK19. Gyles turned back around, scanning, his eyes focused in on the Stryker. The eight-wheeled armored vehicle had a top hatch open and, walking further inside the perimeter, he could see that the back ramp was down. *Why in the hell didn't they button up?* He straightened his body and continued to scan, walking closer. He looked over his shoulder and could see that Mega had the MK19 off the tripod and was cradling it in his arms while Weaver carried two large cans of ammo. They were moving back toward the Humvee. Gyles shifted his position to cover them, watching as they dropped off the weapon and then returned to ferry more ammo back to the vehicle.

He heard a static popping and hissing like the sound of running water and put a hand up. The men were on the return leg of an ammo run when they saw him and froze. Weaver stared at him and showed his palms to ask *what's up?*

Gyles touched his ear and then pointed at the Stryker. He raised his rifle and shuffled toward the static pops. As he got closer, he could hear the tinny pops of a man's voice. They crackled and snapped in a tin resonance. He moved to the rear ramp of the Stryker, swiveling his head to ensure that Weaver and Mega were still behind him. He closed in on the step that led to the rear of the armored vehicle. Looking in, he could see why it hadn't been secured. The troops had been using it as an ambulance, a triage center. The floor of the vehicle was covered with bloody bandages.

He clenched his jaw and looked to where a dead man lay inside with his throat opened up. He hadn't seen someone turn from the infection, but he imagined how it must have happened. He closed his eyes and heard the crackled voice again. It was from a radio. He looked back at Weaver, who recognized the same thing. Now energized, he moved up the ramp and into the vehicle. Below the open hatch was a radio station and a handset dangling from a cord. Gyles heard a man speaking. *"...heavy casualties, request immediate resupply, we need ammo, supplies—"* Gyles put the handset to his ear and said, "Any station, any station, this is India Two-Six. Over."

There was a long pause, but the radio traffic grew silent, which Gyles took as a good sign that he'd been heard. "Any station, any station, this is India Two-Six. Over," he said again.

"India Two-Six this is Anvil One-One. You are on the wrong net, please make your correction. Over."

"Anvil One-One, we are..." He looked at Weaver, suddenly at a loss for words.

"Fuck it, tell them everything," Weaver said. "Get us the hell out of here."

"You are what, India Two-Six. Send your traffic. Over."

"Anvil One-One, this is India Two-Six. We are in the wind. I don't know what's going on. We've lost our company. I have thirty-five souls in my camp, including civilian survivors. No communication with command, we have nowhere to go, we need immediate assistance. Over."

"Wait one, India Two-Six. Over." The radio snapped and returned to static.

"They are going to want to know where we are at." Gyles panicked. They didn't have a map or a GPS, but he still had the notebook with the interstate and highway mile marker on it.

"India Two-Six, this is Anvil One-One. Request full SITREP. Over."

Gyles looked back at Weaver. "A situation report... I just told them we are completely fucked, what else do they want to know?" he said.

Holding his hands up, Weaver shook his head. "Request an extraction."

Gyles smiled at the absurdity of it. "Anvil One-

One. This is India Two-Six with 3rd Infantry Division out of Fort Stewart. My unit is down to six soldiers. We are with survivors of the 147th Aviation and local civilian survivors. We need immediate extraction; we have civilians that we need to get out."

"Negative, India Two-Six. We have no assets available."

"No assets?" He was tired and out of patience. "Listen, we need help. My company is gone. I have people here, and we need help."

"This is Colonel Ericson, who am I speaking with?"

Weaver leaned closer. "Shit—Ericson. I know that name, he's the boss over at Hunter Army Airfield."

"Colonel, this is Sergeant First Class Robert Gyles."

"Listen to me, Sergeant. There is no help out there. Nobody is coming for you. Do you understand that?"

Gyles's heart thudded heavily in his chest, and his stomach retched. He took a deep breath and swallowed, speaking with his voice cracking. "I... I understand, sir. What are my orders?"

"You are on your own. If you are with the Third, the division is in a rolling retreat from Fort Belvoir. They are getting ready for a second assault to take back the city."

"Take back," Gyles mumbled before hitting the transmit button. "Sir, we heard reports that Fort Belvoir is gone. Do we go anyway?"

"Not gone, but they are in a bad way." The radio paused, the static popping before Erickson came back

on the line. *"Listen, son, you do what you need to do for your people, but my best advice is to dig in where you are at. Anyone still in the fight right now is circling the wagons. Nobody will be able to help you if you get out on the roads alone."*

"Understood, sir," Gyles said, lying. "What about Stewart and Hunter?"

"Stewart is in bad shape, Hunter is locked down. I can't send anyone after you." There was a long pause, Gyles thought the connection had dropped before Erikson's voice came back with, *"Good luck, India Two-Six. Anvil One-One out."*

The radio popped and Gyles went to lower the volume before hearing a clatter outside—the sounds of metal falling and clanging onto the surface of the road. He knew what it must have been before having to ask. He looked back at Weaver, who was already on his rifle. The sights to his eye, the man's hand flipped the selector switch to fire.

"Wait," Gyles said, knowing the gunshot would bring on a frenzy.

Weaver pulled the trigger.

CHAPTER EIGHTEEN

DAY OF INFECTION PLUS TEN, 1830 HOURS

Interstate 81, Virginia.

"Fuck, fuck, fuck!" Gyles yelled, climbing over the vehicle's commander seat, pulling himself through the open hatch and onto the roof. He looked out over the back of the vehicle and could see that Weaver had put down two infected charging at them from the rear. From the elevated position he could now see that the tiny perimeter was egg-shaped, completely walled in with a gate at each end. This spot was well-built, and textbook for a perimeter defense against a hostile force. They had sound walls and secure firing positions. But this wasn't a conventional enemy they were facing. He scanned the openings.

The gate on their end was open, the rear gate sealed by a large HEMTT. The things were trying to get past it but were instead pushing themselves up and over the wire around it. He heard Mega shout below.

The man was trying to work the controls to close the back ramp. "Stryker's hosed!" Mega shouted. "There's juice in the battery but not enough to start it, and the ramp is jammed."

He turned back to spot six bloodied faces pouring in from the back of the perimeter. Gyles raised his rifle and fired, stepping closer to the back of the Stryker as he moved. Weaver was already out and down below, firing away with Mega by his side. Gyles saw the immediate threats to the front go down. The things were surrounding the perimeter, the roars growing closer to them; they had to move before they were cut off from the Humvee.

"Leave everything, bound back to the Hummer!" Gyles ordered. He reached down for a handhold on the top edge of the STRYKER and took a hard swing to the ground. Hitting harder than he expected, he rolled forward and flattened out on the blacktop. Pushing up and rolling to his side, he was surprised by a mob closing in on him. "Where in the hell did they come from?" He pushed back and opened fire from his hip. Hitting the first two before the third collided with him. Weaver was quickly beside him. The soldier kicked the third infected loose, landing a boot strike under its chin that echoed with a sickening snap.

Gyles rolled and went to get to his knees, his weapon up and in action. Before he could place his feet and stand, Mega had him by the handle sewn into the back of his gear, dragging him. "Let go, you big bastard! I can walk, damn it."

Mega ignore him, charging toward the vehicle like a runaway bronco, firing his rifle in his left hand, dragging his platoon sergeant with his right. The big man charged ahead, screaming obscenities, not stopping until he reached the driver's door. He released the harness with a twist, causing Gyles to tumble to his side. Again, he found himself clawing at the ground and rising to his knees. Infected were moving it at them from all angles now. Weaver, who had been firing, reached out with an open hand and swung open the passenger side door. "Let's get the fuck out of here!" he shouted.

Gyles nodded. Already back to his feet, he pressed his back against the fender, ahead of the front passenger door. With his weapon up, he rapid fired into a straight line of infected charging directly at him. They dropped like lemmings, his rounds tearing through multiple bodies at a time. As the infected dropped, they tripped up others in the line behind them. He heard the Humvee engine roar to life, and looking over his left shoulder, he could see that Mega was back in the driver's seat.

"Move boss!" Weaver shouted behind him as the rear door slammed shut.

Gyles stepped back and dropped into the vehicle with the other men, latching the door moments before the impacts. The bodies collided with the steel. Looking through the armored front windshield, he could see nothing but a flurry of activity. A face missing its bottom lip was pressed against the glass, the teeth bending and scraping against the armored wind-shield as others behind it pushed the jaw against it. He heard them on the roof, clawing at the turret hatch and screaming against the thick glass embedded in the doors.

Mega dropped the vehicle into reverse and eased on the accelerator. The vehicle hardly moved. He pushed harder, and it surged back, crunching over crea-tures. Bodies were pressed against them on all sides; they were in a sea of death. "Where are you going? You can't see shit!"

"I remember where we were. I made sure it was clear to turn around before I parked us that way," Mega said.

"Maybe you aren't such a shit driver after all."

"Thank you, Sergeant," Mega shouted.

This time the driver clenched his jaw and mashed the accelerator. He cut the wheel, and the vehicle crunched and vibrated over organic obstacles. He cut the wheel hard again. Gyles cringed, hearing the wheels of the Hummer spinning on bodies. The vehicle listed badly as it picked up speed moving through the mob in a tight turn.

The creatures on the roof lost their grip and began to spill off into the road. Mega cursed them, using every profanity in his book as the bodies rolled across the vehicle's hood. He squeezed the wheel and continued to snake the vehicle in reverse, building speed, before locking the wheels in a screeching halt. He then put it back into drive and slammed the pedal again, racing them forward. With a pair of creatures clutching the hood snarling at him, Mega laughed like a psycho and swerved left and right, dislodging the last two from the hood.

Free of the mob and approaching the tangled mess of traffic, Mega stopped cursing. He slowed further to make his way back onto the path they took on the way there. The big man took in labored breaths, a large vein poking from his neck. Weaver leaned between the seats, handing him a bottle of water. "Damn, brother, road rage much? Hope you don't drive your momma's minivan like that."

Mega snatched the bottle and poured half over his head before chugging the rest. "Sergeant, tell me we aren't never going back there," Mega gasped. "No more interstates, no more fucking places like that."

Gyles had his eyes closed and was clenching his rifle to his chest, muscles still twitching with adrenaline. "Yeah, we're done with that shit, Mega. Just get us back to the camp," he said.

Weaver moved equipment and cans into the center of the vehicle. In his haste, he'd jumped in the wrong door and was crammed in against the MK19 and several cans of ammo. He dug himself out then pushed several cans to the middle. Gyles looked back. "How'd we score?" he asked. "Did we get enough ammo?"

"Four cans of 5.56, two cans of 7.62, and about a hundred and twenty-five for the MK19. Oh shit, boss, take a look at this," he said, holding up a large canvas bag. It was long, holding the shape of a woman's shopping bag. "I thought it was a tool bag when I grabbed it." He held the bag open. Inside were a dozen storage tubes for M67 fragmentation grenades. Gyles reached in and took one of the tubes. Prying it open, he grinned. "That'll do, pig, that'll do." He laughed as he stuck a pair of the grenades into empty pouches on his vest.

CHAPTER NINETEEN

DAY OF INFECTION PLUS 10, 2055 HOURS

Interstate 81, Virginia.

As requested, they didn't go near the farm on the return leg, and by the time they passed the corner store, the forest was growing dark. Mega asked about the headlights, and Gyles shook his head no. They couldn't risk white light; there were too many things to consider. For the moment they hadn't seen any of the infected after making the turn back onto the county road at the intersection. There were a scattered few moving in that direction, but they hoped the things would continue and not make the turn toward the national forest.

He'd seen them in action several times now, and he was convinced there wasn't anything Luke would be able to do to the camp to defend against a horde. And he knew that eventually a horde would come. It would start in ones and twos, but they would fire their weapons, and more would come, then every damn thing in the valley would be moving toward them. There would be no place to go, and with a large convoy they might not be able to outrun an advance. Or worse, they might find themselves running into even more.

Gyles held his breath, watching Mega make a turn onto the narrow roadway that would lead them back to the campground. He could see that the men had been busy. There were boxes of supplies stacked in the parking area. The pickets had been expanded, and all the windows completely secured on the cabins. Humvees were parked at the corners of the compounds, and the two MRAPs flared at the gate parked in a way that one could back up and completely seal the entrance, yet still allow people to board the rear ramps.

It would be hard to convince people to leave here. Maybe just as hard to convince others to stay. Colonel Erickson told him to dig in and protect his people, that the fight was lost. But his division was fighting and dying somewhere to the north. He was part of them; it was his job to get back to his people. No, his people were here. He shook his head and looked toward the window as Mega pulled into the end of the gravel lot. "What's up, G-Man? I see you stressing up there," Weaver said.

"Just been a long day, brother. Let's unass this steel box," he said, swinging the door out and stepping into the cool twilight. The temperatures were dropping, and the humidity had finally faded to where he wasn't sweating standing still. He moved to the front of the Humvee and placed his rifle on the hood. He leaned against it and watched Weaver and Mega walk toward the cabins. Halfway there they were greeted by Luke and Rose. They exchanged words and the two men continued the walk down the path toward him.

"You did good on the recon," Luke said, pointing to the boxes. "We're working on breaking everything down and packing it into the armored vehicles."

Gyles nodded his agreement. "We found more than that."

"Yeah, I kind of got that idea from the looks on your men's faces. I take it the rest of the day didn't go well," Luke said.

"No, it didn't," Gyles said, shaking his head. "I think we may be stuck here for a while."

"That might be a problem," Luke said. The man turned and glanced at Rose standing beside him with his hands in his pockets.

"You should show him," Rose said.

"Show me what?" Gyles asked.

Luke grimaced and turned, walking away. Rose signaled for Gyles to follow. He sighed and grabbed his rifle from the hood and followed the men away from the lot and into the tree line. When they'd gotten ten feet from the grass and into the thicker foliage, they were greeted by a soldier with a hood pulled down over his brow. His rifle was slung over his back, and he was caring a sharpened pike across the front of his body. When he saw the group approach, he pulled up the hood. Gyles recognized him as one of the riflemen from First Squad, Specialist Culver. He was a grunt from Illinois, good kid, always reliable in a fight. Gyles moved up next to him and stopped with the others.

"What you got going on out here, Culver?" Gyles asked, pointing at the man's spear. On first impression, that was what Gyles thought Luke wanted to show him. That his troopers were already going *Lord of the Flies* only a few days into this.

That thought vanished when the young soldier turned and pointed to a patch of brush off the trail that was pressed down. Gyles took careful steps toward it and stopped. There were at least six corpses stacked up. Gyles turned back and the soldier nodded, no show of pride or shame. It was a matter-of-fact look; the kid's face was hard. Gyles had seen the look plenty of times, in faraway places. Men did what needed to be done, but they took no pleasure in it.

"Those things have been coming up the trail all day. One at a time mostly, but sometimes two, even three," he said.

"You're out here all alone?" Gyles asked.

Culver shook his head. "No, Sergeant. Couple guys are further up the trail, scouting. If they see something coming, they slip back, and we ambush them together with the spears. There is a place just ahead where we hold the high ground, and they must move up to get at us. These things don't do much tactical thinking, so we just pop out and stick 'em."

"And you took these with pikes?" Gyles asked.

Luke grunted and Gyles turned to see the man shaking his head. "A lot more than this. There is another body drop fifty yards up the trail. And we are running another identical setup to this on the backside. No gunfire unless it's life or death; we have to stay quiet." The man looked down and kicked dirt at his feet. "We've put down over twenty of them since lunch."

"They're going to keep coming," Gyles said.

Rose nodded and considered the camp and vehicles in the distance. "We have to plan for it; these trails go for miles. Who knows what's at the other end? Could just be a few stranded cars but could also be a community of them on the march."

Luke stepped closer to the men. "We have some advantages... they seem to like the paths. These things are a lazy. When not attacking, they stick to the easy terrain."

"We also have night vision," Rose added.

"That'll give us an edge as long as their numbers are manageable." Gyles's hands tightened as he thought about the roadblock. "We need a plan to escape when they horde up, because they will." His voice creaked, and the men looked at him. They knew the comment was about more than what had happened at the armory. He took a deep breath and looked back toward the cabins in the distance. "We ran into hundreds of them not even an hour away—possibly thousands. The highway was congested. It looked like civilians were fleeing in every direction and got caught up in something—it was bad."

He paused as scenes from earlier flash in his head. "Listen, if we fire even one shot up here, they'll come in from miles away. This Dawn of Civilization, spears and trenches stuff will work for now, but not with what I saw out there today." He slowly walked away from his spot and tuned back toward the fading daylight. "We found a small encampment—they were tactically dug in, they were prepared, and the things poured over the wall. I mean dug in with machine guns and armor. This camp won't hold. We need a real plan."

Luke rubbed his knuckles against his temple and pointed to the hastily built perimeter fences with vehicles parked in every corner. "We took a quick egress into consideration. None of us want a repeat of what happened at the armory. I have the vehicles parked at holes in the perimeter so they can pull out if needed. The MRAPS are at the gates and ready to go. If we get surrounded, we'll mount up and haul ass. You guys did good on the recon today, all the trucks are topped off and we have cans to spare." He paused and looked down at his boots again. "But with that... When it comes time to pull up stakes. Where do we go?"

"We contacted a colonel at Hunter," Gyles said. He'd planned to give the message later over a full briefing but now seemed as good a time as any.

"Hunter? Are you sure?" Rose asked.

"Yeah, I'm sure. He said they were holding, but not able to send us help."

Luke rubbed his temples. "Then we go to them. If shit here falls apart, we button up and head to Hunter."

"That's a hell of a haul," Rose said. "Five hundred miles even when the roads weren't closed."

"Anything on the Chinook?" Gyles asked.

Rose tipped his head from ear to ear and rolled his hand. "It's good and bad. The pilots found a civilian field inside our flight time that can probably support our refueling."

"Probably?" Gyles asked.

Swallowing, Rose said, "They are on the map as a designated emergency field for the National Guard, but we can't raise them on the radio. Still the place is out of the way from everyone, and they should have fuel."

"But if they don't?"

"Then yeah—no fuel and we'd be in the wind. We'd have to find a plan B and sort it out. Dozens of things could go wrong, but the pilots seem up to the challenge."

Gyles nodded and pointed toward the camp. "So—real question is... do we go on our own terms or wait until these things run us off?"

Luke shrugged. "This can't be permanent either way. The food you brought will last for a minute, but that's not good enough. If this colonel is out there, then we need to link up as soon as we're able or at first sign of trouble."

"You've all done a lot of work here; you think folks will be open to leaving?"

Luke smiled. "You know the rules of defense, you dig in and continually improve your position until it's time to bug out. You can't get attached to your hole, or you'll end up being buried in it."

The platoon sergeant smiled. He'd heard that same lecture plenty of times in the field after digging out the perfect bunker to only have word come down that the company was moving a hundred meters to the left. "Okay, as soon as we're packed and ready we go. Same with the Chinook. I'll leave it on the crew if you want to take the risk or convoy out with us. But we all need to be on the alert and ready to jump."

The men nodded agreements. Before Gyles could turn away, Luke pointed at the front of his uniform, covered with blood and gore. "When are you going to get yourself cleaned up and grab some chow?" he said. "We don't have time for any John Wayne stuff out here. You need to take care of yourself, so we can take care of the others."

Gyles raised his hands in mock surrender. "You won't get any arguments out of me; point me in the right direction, and I'll gladly grab a hot and a cot." He stopped and looked back to Culver, who was pulling his hood back over the top of his head. "These guys going to be okay out here?"

Luke nodded. "I have them rotating out every hour. If it gets too shady, I'll pull them all back inside the wire, and we'll take our chances at hiding."

Apprehensively, Gyles let his eyes sweep the forest terrain again. He didn't like the idea of his men being outside with fighting sticks, but the alternative was to let the infected slowly stack up against them. Even if it was just pounding corks into a dam, they had to do something to hold back the flood. He put a hand on Luke's shoulder then turned to move back toward the main cabin. He saw a work party was hastily bringing the rest of the boxes inside or stuffing them into already overfilled vehicles. The black truck and trailer had also joined the convoy, the trailer now carefully filled with goods. Even the red Toyota pickup with the shot-out windows was in the lot, the bed stuffed with goods.

He moved closer to the cabin, winding around the fence line made of sharpened stakes. At the opening, he was greeted by a man with a police tactical vest, holding an axe. He gave Gyles a half wave and moved back a wooden gate to let him in. The dirt trail led up to the covered porch of the main cabin. Forty feet wide and at least sixty deep, it was obviously built as a bunk house, while the two cabins located on each side were smaller, thirty-by-thirty squares and more private.

The smaller ones to the left and right were shuttered with doors open. Gyles could hear children's voices from the building to the left. Men were moving hastily to load boxes of goods into the building on the right. The daylight was fading fast, and the camp was preparing for darkness. A pair of women were standing outside the main cabin. They hushed their conversation when he approached. Gyles passed the women, dipping his chin to them in greeting and moved into the main cabin.

Inside the door and along the near wall was a table with food items scattered along it. At the end was a cast iron kettle filled with a mixture of what looked like beans and bits of beef jerky. Next to that, a stack of water bottles. He shook his head and loaded a plastic bowl. Taking a small taste, he found it was cold, but it didn't force a gag reflex, so he filled his bowl to the top and dropped a handful of crackers into the mix. He snatched a bottle of water.

"How's the headache?"

Gyles looked over his shoulder and saw his medic, Rodriguez, sitting at a table with Doctor Howard. He tried to hold back a scowl, not excited to have one of his junior troops being influenced by the man. He sighed and moved to the table, leaning his rifle against the wall behind him and sat across from the two medical men. "It's better, thanks for asking, Doc."

He saw Howard roll his eyes at Gyles calling the junior medic a doc. Gyles smiled and took a spoonful of the cold bean soup. He looked toward the back of the room and could see cots set up and tables converted to beds. Even though he'd only been away from the camp a few hours, they'd made many improvements to the place. It looked like the entire group could sleep in here if they had to. Men were already asleep in several of the racks.

Rodriguez noticed him inspecting. "Luke moved all the bunks in here, he says it's better if we're all in one place if we have to move fast or barricade inside. The cabin on the right is a store room and the one on the left a sort of HQ."

Gyles nodded. "I heard kids in there."

Laughing, Rodriguez nodded. "We let them play in there, keeps them out of trouble—and out of here so the night guards can get their sleep during the day."

"They shouldn't even be here," Howard grunted. "You should take them someplace; we don't have the means to be caring for children."

Surprised by the comment, Gyles looked at the man. "Where exactly do we do that?"

"They should have landed that helicopter and not been turned around again." The doctor shook his head. "What the hell are we doing out here, anyway? Camping? Do you plan to keep us here?"

Gyles flashed a bright smile and shoveled in another spoonful of the grub, staring down Howard as he slowly chewed. He heard the door behind him open as more men entered the room and loaded more bowls. He picked up on their conversations. The men were talking about the skirmish at the military roadblock. Word was traveling fast, not hard when Mega didn't know how to whisper. One of the National Guard soldiers noticed Gyles at the table and moved closer. Gyles could tell the man had something to say.

"Get on with it," Gyles said, looking at the trooper.

The man shrugged and shook his head. "It's nothing, Sergeant."

Gyles softened his expression. "Really, it's okay."

The man looked down at his bowl and said, "I was just wondering if we could try and go back to Vines."

Not expecting that question, he looked up at the man. "You want to go back?"

"Well, I was just thinking, if all those people—" he stopped and looked back down at his bowl. "Well, if all those things were out on the highway, they had to come from someplace. Maybe Vines is cleared out now."

Howard cleared his throat and spoke up in a different tone, sounding more like a college professor, than the whining he'd done earlier. "It would be logical to assume that the infected would move toward populated areas. Depending on the behavior of the infected, of course."

"Behavior?" Gyles asked, "We've seen the behavior; they kill everything in sight."

"Behavior may be a simplistic way to say it. Let's say characteristics... or motivations," Howard said.

Rodriguez raised his eyebrows. "Motivations... like what do they need?"

Howard smiled and looked at the medic like a star pupil. "Precisely. What is it they *need*."

Gyles pursed his lips. He wasn't liking the impact the doctor was having on his only medic; it could be troublesome. He could see that the table's occupants had all changed focus and were now looking at the doctor with interest. He would have to deal with Howard's fraternization with the men later. He grunted. "Needs." Gyles lifted a spoon full of the beans and showed it for effect. "They need to eat."

"That's one thing, but there may be others," Howard said. "We do know that this disease shares traits with the rabies virus that attacks the central nervous system. Originally, we assumed these things would behave as *rabid* creatures. Often predators with rabies will not feed. The disease progresses and attacks the brain. Eventually the infected wither and die.

"We already know from observations that these creatures do in fact feed. But they have another motivation. They are not just mad in a mental sense. We do know from—" Howard stopped speaking. He seemed to realize he was talking to a table full of soldiers and not colleagues at the Centers for Disease Control.

Gyles put up his hand. "We do know what?"

Howard looked away. "It's still highly classified; the research and clinical studies haven't been released. I probably shouldn't."

Laughing, Gyles said, "I would say we are in the center of a clinical study, Doctor, and if you ever want to be able to release your findings, you should start sharing your information."

Howard looked at Gyles. "Most of this is just conjecture, as the European offices went dark before they could present their findings."

"If it can help us, we need to know," Gyles said. He wished Luke and the others were here, but he didn't want to risk the man shutting up.

Howard looked at the others at the table, stopping at Rodriquez, who stared back as if the doctor was an all-knowing professor. The looks of the men were enough to stoke his ego into continuing. "Patients captured in the field showed early signs of needing to spread the virus. It appeared to be the primary motivation. They would bypass obvious food sources to get at the uninfected. They had some need to completely occupy a region. During this process they grouped together and swarmed over their regions, trying to infect everything within their bubble. Once they went a period of hours without contact with the uninfected, their mentality adjusted—adjusted quite rapidly, in fact.

"In the absence of threats, or the uninfected, they developed a hive mentality. Their physical activity dropped, almost completely stopping during daylight hours. This is when the first transition occurred. They grouped together and the motivations switched to feeding, then when they did feed it was like pack hunters. They would kill and return the kills to their hives."

"Pack hunters?" Gyles asked "Like wolves?"

"The European researchers compared them to predatory birds. They flock together and hunt in massive waves, in mobbing attacks. But yes, wolves would be the same. They will bunch up and hunt at night; most daytime attacks will be chance encounters."

Gyles raised his eyebrows. At the laboratory, the attack was in the dark. At the armory, the attack was at sundown. "Why hunt at night?"

"Their eyes," Howard said. "These things have suffered severe brain damage. Part of what we have observed is a lack of pupillary response. They are nearly blind in bright light." The doctor looked down the table at confused faces. He smiled. "The light is too bright for their eyes; they can't adjust to it. They will spend a lot of the daytime hiding or staying in the shadows. But at night, yes they will hunt and attack under the cover of darkness."

"They are smart? They can hunt us?" one of the soldiers asked.

Howard shook his head. "It's hard to say; we never got that far. With the early understanding of the disease, there is nothing to say that the infected cannot continue to evolve. There is nothing in the Primalis Rabia virus itself to cause death to the host. In fact, the opposite seems to be true. Once the infected body adjusts to the virus it becomes stronger and harder to kill. It was far too early in our research to see the full effects on the brain and what these things may eventually become."

Gyles put up his finger. "Then let me ask. Vines—today would the city be empty? Or would they be hiving there?"

Howard grimaced and looked toward the men at the table. "Early evidence would suggest that once the population was completely infected, they would hive. The city will never be safe again, unless we moved in and killed them all."

CHAPTER TWENTY

GW National Forest, Virginia.

"Sergeant Gyles." A light shone down brightly into his face. His hand reached for this sidearm tucked against his hip. Gyles blinked away the blindness, and the soldier pulled the light away. "Sergeant, they need you next door."

Grunting, Gyles pulled himself up and threw his legs over the side of the cot. He squinted again and strained his eyes, considering the face of a National Guard private—the man was holding a spear, his rifle slung across his back. Then he looked down at his wristwatch. "Damn, son, this better be good."

The private nodded. "Sergeant Weaver said to wake you up right away."

"Where is he?" he asked, leaning down to strap on his boots.

"Next door in HQ cabin."

Gyles stood and looked around the cabin. A low light glowed from the front. Men snored in cots along the walls and sides, while family members and children were clustered in the center of the floor at the back of the cabin. He holstered his sidearm and reached for his rifle then waved his hand for the private to lead the way. The man darted off ahead, seemingly relieved to be away from him. Gyles followed and exited through the front door.

The air was cold and damp, a heavy fog hung thick on the ground. He felt the chill on his neck and back and pulled the collar closed on his jacket. He looked out into the fog, seeing nothing but the thick drifting mist, the light of the moon causing it to glow. He could see men positioned in the turrets of the Humvees at the corners of the perimeter. They wore night vision devices that were flipped up on top of their heads. He heard the door open to the cabin next door and turned to enter it.

As he wearily walked inside, a solider handed him a cup of coffee with steam coming off the top. He went to blow on the hot cup and froze when he spotted the couple sitting on folding metal chairs in the corner. A man in mud-stained blue jeans and a puffy blue jacket. A female wearing a hip-length wool coat and tight-fitting khaki pants. On the ground at their feet was a small navy-blue knapsack and a large carryall bag. Gyles raised his eyebrows and pointed at the couple sitting in the corner, staring at him with sheepishly large eyes.

Weaver was standing near a table, looking over a large tactical map of the area. Gyles looked around the room. Luke wasn't there and neither were Rose or the pilots. He moved closer to Weaver and tipped his head toward the strangers. "That why you woke me?"

Weaver nodded, continuing his stare toward the map for a second longer before he looked up. "Meet Nicole and Kyle," he said, turning toward the pair.

The woman's eyes stayed wide, unresponsive to the words. The man leaned forward. His face was covered with dirty black streaks around his eyes and under his nose. He wore a days' old beard, and his cheeks were gaunt. Gyles took a step toward the man and the man flinched back, leaning into his chair. Gyles stopped and stepped away, leaning against the table instead, giving the couple plenty of room. "And where exactly did Nicole and Kyle come from?"

Kyle put his hands over his face and rubbed at his eyes. "We need to leave, why did your people take us here?" the man said, mumbling. The woman beside him cowered at the sound of his voice, not in a way that she feared him, but that she feared everything.

Weaver moved closer and handed the man an already open bottle of water. "Our soldiers took you here because they found you wandering alone on the trail. You know we've been killing infected on that trail all night."

The man took the bottle and drank from it. "We can't stay here; it isn't safe," he said. He turned and grabbed the woman's arm then eased the bottle into her hands. She looked up at him with glassed-over eyes and put the bottle to her lips.

"Is she okay?" Gyles asked.

The man glared back at him. "Are any of us okay?"

Gyles turned back to the private. "Go get Doctor Howard," he said. The private turned and left the room. He looked back at the man. "Now listen... Kyle, right? I don't know what you think of us, but we aren't the bad guys here. We just want to know who you are. If, after that, you still feel the need to get back on the road, we'll put you right back where we found you." Gyles looked up and could see frustration on Weaver's face.

Kyle reached into a small pocket on the sleeve of his jacket and pulled out a folded sheet of paper. "We were going here," he said and handed it to Gyles.

The paper was printed in black ink and held both Red Cross and FEMA symbols on the bottom. There was a list of city names that Gyles recognized in Georgia. But it was Atlanta at the top that was circled in blue ink. It said that shelter, food, and security were available and encouraged anyone not able to shelter at home to go there.

"You went to Atlanta?" he asked.

"We tried. Others like you stopped us, told us to go west. Then they shot and bombed us anyway," Kyle said. "We had to leave our car on the interstate and take to the forest. But—" The man set his jaw and looked toward the entrance. "Listen, we can't stay here. Please let us go."

"You said 'but.' What were you going to say?" Gyles asked.

Kyle looked at the woman next to him; her head was pressed into his shoulder now, her eyes closed and her breathing heavy. He seemed relieved that the woman was resting. He closed his own eyes and sighed before slowly opening them again. "It's just—it's just been so much and so fast. I don't even know what day it is."

Weaver moved a chair closer and held a cup of coffee in his hands. With his voice calm he asked, "How long have you been on the road?"

Exhaling through pursed lips, the man closed his eyes. He opened them and looked up toward the ceiling. "Three days... wait, no four days. We were with friends, we tried for Atlanta, but the highway was backed up. People slept in their cars, and finally the soldiers came. They walked right down the interstate, telling us we needed to turn around and go west, that everything east of the Appalachians wasn't safe."

"The Appalachians, that's the entire East Coast," Gyles said. "Are you sure?"

Kyle nodded. "I didn't believe it either. Nobody did." He drank from his bottle of water again. "The soldier told us the only camps holding were in Texas and Colorado. There is something going on up North by Michigan, but it's cut off by the fighting. Most of the Army is still in the Capital, trying to fight it out, and it's drawing in more of the infected. They said the Army was still holding at Fort Knox, Kentucky, if we could get there."

"Did you leave?"

"We stayed. Lots of us did. The soldiers patrolled the line of cars every morning, handing out food and water, telling us every time that we needed to move west. But on the third morning... Yesterday morning they didn't. That's when it started. There were no soldiers that morning."

"The infected?" Gyles asked.

"I didn't see any infected at first. It was in the afternoon. We could hear the fighting far away. Then people began to panic. They ran from the north, moving down the highway, carrying everything they had." He stopped and took in a breath. "Then the helicopters—more helicopters than I have seen in my life— they flew directly north and then the sky turned black with smoke.

"It got quiet; we thought maybe it was over. People left their cars and started to walk south. We waited; I didn't know what else to do. I thought maybe the soldiers would come back."

Gyles leaned in. "Did they?"

Kyle shook his head no. "The sun went down and then it happened. The people outside the cars were no longer walking; they were running, and then the screams came. The screams were so loud, you couldn't hear the gunfire." Kyle froze, his hand squeezing the bottle. "I was able to get Nicole from the car. People were running at us... the crowds and the screaming... People were being attacked by the infected. People were trying to fight them. Some just froze. We got separated from our friends. I pulled her up the embankment toward the tree line. Then the real killing started; the infected mixed with the rest of us. The soldiers had finally arrived.

"There was no relief. They opened fire from armored vehicles. I couldn't believe it, they just shot into the crowds. I grabbed Nicole and I ran. I ran and didn't look back. Even when we heard the explosions, I didn't look." He closed his eyes and let his head slump.

"Maybe that's enough," Gyles said. "Let's give him some space until the doctor has a look at them."

"No," Kyle said, his head coming back up. "They are close—we don't have time for that. We weren't alone in the woods. The infected followed us. There were a lot of us in the woods last night. I hid Nicole the best I could, but I heard them attacking and killing all night. When the sun came up, we ran for the hills. Literally. We just kept running for the high ground. That was when we bumped into your men."

The door opened and Doctor Howard entered, pausing when he saw the strangers. He went to speak but stopped when Gyles held up his hand.

"How many?"

"Infected?" Kyle said. "Too many; you can't count that many. And every time we stopped, we heard them. They are close."

Gyles stood and turned to Weaver. "Wake Luke and the others. We're bugging out."

"Going where?" Howard asked.

Still not ready to take questions or demands from the doctor, Gyles turned back. He was trying to co-exist with the self-serving coward, but that relationship was still a long way off. Gyles hardened his stare and delivered an ad hoc plan. "The aircrew is going to leapfrog to a civilian station to attempt to top off then make for Hunter Army Airfield, from there I don't know."

"Then that's where I am going," Howard said. "I have to get back to the laboratories in Maryland."

Gyles grinned. "Have at it."

"What about the rest of us?" Weaver asked.

"Just before dawn we'll do like the man says—pack everything up and point the civilians and law enforcement folks east."

"What about the rest of us?" Weaver said again.

Gyles grimaced. "I'm taking as many willing to go back toward Fort Belvoir. There is still a fight out there."

CHAPTER TWENTY-ONE

DAY OF INFECTION PLUS ELEVEN, 0515 HOURS

GW National Forest, Virginia.

The infected were at the walls before the last vehicle was loaded. Gyles swiftly walked back to the cabins. He could hear the gunfire. His men were providing cover for the aircrew. The blades were already turning and the big turbines spun up. He saw Weaver leaving the large building, and the man gave him a thumbs up. "Everyone is out. We are all loaded up."

"Okay. Mount up. I'm right behind you," Gyles shouted, moving back to take one last sweep of the compound as the gunfire intensified behind him. He had to ensure nobody was left behind. Satisfied, he turned and ran to the back ramp of the MRAP, moving inside. The big hatch clanked shut behind him as he stepped inside. He moved up to the front and slapped the back of the driver's seat. "Take us out of here."

Luke nodded and the big armored vehicle lurched forward slowly toward the gravel lot. As they moved, the other armored vehicles pulled away from their positions in the wall and joined the long iron snake that was slowly forming on the road. Gyles heard the gunfire and pointed to a headset plugged into the roof of the MRAP. Most of the vehicle's radios still weren't plugged into the outside world, but they had managed to get internal communications up.

Luke pulled down a handset and passed it to Gyles. "We're Reapers now."

"Reapers?" Gyles asked, his eyebrows going up.

"Hey, the kids liked it." Luke laughed, easing the big vehicle over ruts.

Gyles nodded and held the handset to his face. "All Reaper elements, this is Reaper Six. Button up and cease fire; they can't get at you inside the vehicles. Keep an eye on those civilian trucks. If they need help, get after them." He let go of the transmission button and counted the responses as each one of the vehicles in the convoy checked in. He looked from the window and saw the swirling dust as the Chinook ripped away from the ground and raced for the civilian airfield less than fifty miles to their east.

The CH-47 took four of the guardsmen with them for flight crew and security, giving them a crew of nine and leaving twenty-six bodies with the convoy. Gyles hoped it would be enough. It was no surprise to him that once Doctor Howard realized the nature of the Chinook's mission that he would not be going with them. The men going with the helo gave them more room in the vehicles and less mouths to feed on the convoy. But now they also had less shooters.

Wondering what to do next, Gyles sat back in the seat. Things were so much easier when he had a command telling him what to do. It was against doctrine to split up their forces, and that was exactly what he was about to do.

He looked up over the console. Luke had the map laid out and a large area circled in red. The initial goal was to break contact with the infected, move swiftly down the gravel roads until they lost them. Then Luke would take the convoy to a pre-determined rally point, which on the map was identified as a large parking lot near a trailhead. If by chance any of the vehicles were separated from the convoy, they would meet at the parking lot.

The cupola's viewing port, where the salvaged MK19 grenade launcher was now mounted, allowed in a view on all sides of the vehicle. It was still dark; the trucks were running with their lights on, as there were not enough night vision devices to go around. Gyles's vehicle led the convoy, with two Humvees directly behind them, and the second MRAP behind those. As they moved past the trees, there were no signs of the infected along the shoulder of the roads. They were alone.

When the truck slowed and turned west, Gyles moved to the front. Luke pointed at the map. "We'll be coming up on the approach road soon."

Gyles lifted the handset. "All Reaper elements, this is Reaper Six. We're coming into the lot. Circle the wagons and kill the engines for a listening stop." He reached to the front and clipped the handset back to the console then watched through the windshield as the MRAP made a turn onto a narrow drive that quickly widened. The sun was rising and Gyles could see down the road. There was a pair of abandoned small cars near a national forest sign. Luke slowed as he drove past them. "Hikers," he said. "This was a popular spot to leave your car when backpacking."

The road got wider ahead and leveled out into a large picnic area that overlooked a lake. Luke took the MRAP close then cut the wheel, forming a large arc until he spotted the tail vehicle. He pulled past it and stopped. The rest of the vehicles slowly did the same, facing out. Headlights were extinguished and engines turned off. Very quickly, the area was void of sound. Gyles took the radio again and hit the transmit button. "All Reaper elements, this is Reaper Six. Check in. Over."

He held the handset, listening to the all-clear from each vehicle before saying, "Get comfortable and hang tight. Let's make sure we're alone. Reaper Six out."

He re-clipped the radio to the console then moved back to the cupola. He unlatched the hatch and let it open before he rose up into damp morning air. A heavy bank of fog hung over the lake. The trees were thin here, and he could see at least fifty yards into the forest. Slowly, he turned his body and checked the entire area before dropping back into the hatch. Moving to the front, he looked at Luke. "Any word form Rose?" They had no open communications with the military from their vehicles, but the Chinook could communicate to the police equipment they had on board.

Luke shook his head. "I'll keep checking. If all went well, they should be finishing up their refueling operation about now." He turned in his seat. "You sure about going to Belvoir?"

Gyles shrugged. "I'm not sure about much of anything anymore. All of this has me questioning everything."

"Then go west," Luke said.

"I can't—if the Third is still fighting, I have to get back to them."

"What about the others? The other soldiers?"

"I'll give them a choice. If they want to go west, they can," Gyles said.

"You know that isn't a choice. They'll go wherever you go."

Gyles rubbed his chin and looked down. "We'll find out soon enough. Can your officers stand the watch while I talk to the troopers?"

"We got it," Luke said. He called back to Gyles as the man turned away. "Gyles, I'm going with you. And so is The Beast."

Gyles looked at him. "Why?"

"I got people in North Carolina; I'm not ready to give up on them yet."

Gyles nodded and exited the back hatch to move to the center of the large circle. Weaver saw him and left the Humvee he was riding in near the back. Gyles waited for his friend to get close then said, "I'm going to Belvoir."

"Yeah, I thought you might."

Gyles chewed at his lip. "What about the troops? What do they want to do?"

"It's mixed, G-Man. We all got friends and family back at Stewart. But these kids—they got family all over the country. I think if you ask them to go with you, they will."

"I don't want to ask them; I want them to volunteer."

Weaver smiled as he fished into his pocket and removed a can of tobacco. He shoved a patch in his jaw and said, "Well, it's hard to say then. They aren't connected to these civilians the way they are to you, Sergeant."

Gyles smiled, hearing Weaver call him by his rank. He knew the conversation was changing. "This isn't an order. I really need them to want to be on board, or to just go west with the others."

"Hell—we don't know what's west. We supposed to trust the word of some busted up guy and a mute chick? If it was up to me, boss, you'd just say to hell with Fort Belvoir and help get these people to safety."

"You know I can't do that."

"Can't... or won't?"

Gyles looked down and slowly slung his head left to right. "The rest of the company, the rest of the battalion might be at Belvoir slugging it out. Men we bled with in Iraq might be there."

"They might all be dead," Weaver said. "You heard Erickson; he said take care of your people."

Gyles removed his helmet and ran his hand through his hair, clenching his eyes tight. He looked back at his friend, trying to keep his voice calm, even though he could feel the tightness in his chest pulling at him. "I just can't do it, Weaver. I can't just abandon them, not knowing."

"I know you can't, boss. It's shit like this why you got the platoon, and I'm still a squad leader."

"The platoon is gone," Gyles said, his voice breaking.

Weaver shook his head. "No, we're still here. Come on, let's get this over with; we've got places to be."

Gyles took a deep breath and looked at his men waiting near a vehicle. He pointed at his collar and made a lasso motion. Soon all seven of the surviving platoon members were moving toward him. *No*, he thought, *all seven but one.* He looked toward the waiting vehicles and then back to the faces of his men, then to Weaver. "Where is Specialist Rodriguez?"

Before Weaver could answer, Mega sounded off with his booming voice. "Up in the MRAP, Sarnt."

Gyles shook his head and touched a finger to his ear like it was ringing. "Mega, you've really got to work on that."

The big man frowned and took a step back.

"Why isn't he out here?" Gyles asked then gave a stern point to the big soldier, cautioning him to watch his volume.

Mega grinned, and in a hoarse whisper said, "That doctor wanted him to stay in the truck, said they are too important to be standing around outside where something could get at them."

Gyles turned to Weaver, then shook his head. "Well, maybe the doctor has a point," Gyles said, knowing damn well he didn't, but also not wanting to start a pissing contest in front of his men. He turned and looked back at the circle of vehicles. The police officers were now standing up in the turrets, looking out. He could see Luke in the cupola of the MRAP, standing behind the MK19. Gyles grinned when he noticed someone had tagged the big vehicle with the words *"The Beast"* in red paint above the *Vines City Police Department* logo. With a deep breath, he turned back to his men.

"Listen, we're breaking off here. The CH-47 has made a move of its own to refuel and travel to Hunter. The civilians will be moving west with the police and Guard. Fort Knox is the hope. If not, they'll just keep going until they find someone."

Culver went to say something, and Gyles put up a hand. "I'm going to try and link back up with the battalion at Fort Belvoir. I'm not going to lie; I've been told they are getting their asses kicked up in D.C. That the division may even be gone by the time we get there."

"So, we go with you then, Sergeant," Culver said, this time not being silenced.

"It's an option, but I won't make any of you go. You need to decide what you think is best for you. I can't guarantee that either of these are the best course right now."

"Well, hell, it's a long enough drive to Fort Knox," Mega grunted. "And there is a guy in Third Platoon that still owes me money."

Gyles looked at them. "Listen... grab your gear and meet me by The Beast, if you're in. Otherwise, it's been an honor serving with you. I wish you all the best of luck." He turned and slowly walked back toward the MRAP. Howard was waiting for him when he got there. Rodriguez was standing just behind him. Gyles grinned. There was nothing the doctor could say to set him off. "What's up, Doc?"

"I heard this reckless plan to send the civilians to Fort Knox while the rest of you head off to your deaths in the city. That's a negative. I have to get to Maryland; we still have a mission."

"Do what you want, Doc. Go west with the civvies or head out with us. Take one of those pickup trucks and go to Maryland. I'm not twisting any arms."

"If you go to Belvoir you'll die."

"Probably," Gyles said. He stepped aside as the first of his soldiers approached the MRAP and tied heavy packs to the roof.

"And you're taking all the soldiers too?" Howard scoffed. "Well, you can't have Rodriguez."

Gyles grinned and looked at the specialist. "That's your call. I gave everyone a choice."

"Well, nobody asked me," Howard said, moving closer and puffing out his chest.

Gyles's fist clenched. "You don't have an option. I gave the soldiers a choice. You're a civilian. I suggest you get back to your ride before you lose your seat."

Howard turned and stomped away, moving back toward the second MRAP. Gyles looked at Rodriguez. He could see in the man's eyes that he wanted to follow the doctor. "It's okay, Rodriguez. Those people are going to need you; they'll need a good medic."

"You sure, Sergeant?"

Gyles dipped his chin and waved him off. He watched Rodriguez rush away to follow the doctor, then he turned back toward the MRAP and did a count. Of his nine soldiers, five had decided to go with him. He sighed. It was five more than he'd expected. They were Weaver's boys from First Squad... Culver, Mega, Private O'Riley—a tall lanky farm boy from Iowa—Scott, a corporal who was overdue to make sergeant and was an expert grenadier from Philadelphia, and Sergeant Tucker, a hard-charging noncom from Jersey City. "I'm glad to have you all. Get your gear settled, and we'll be rolling out."

At the front of the MRAP, Gyles saw that Luke was helping men secure gear to the sides as he said his goodbyes to the police officers. Moving close, Gyles said, "Any word from Rose?"

Luke shook his head no. "Nothing, but it could just be the range of the radios."

Gyles set his jaw. "Okay, let the convoy roll out first, then we'll turn and head for the Capital."

CHAPTER TWENTY-TWO

Near Heritage, Virginia.

L eaving the national forest was uneventful. The men were packed into the back of the MRAP, gear piled all around them. Gyles rode in the front with Luke, who refused to let anyone else drive. Looking back, he could see Weaver's lower body. The sergeant had been swapping out with the others for time in the cupola; it gave them an opportunity to stretch their legs. They'd checked in with the other vehicles for the first couple hours until the signal faded as the convoy moved deeper into the Appalachians, and they themselves moved down and out of them.

Luke knew the terrain and the roads. He kept them off the main interstate. Traveling on state highways and county roads would take longer, but the going was easier. They drove through small towns with burning buildings and smoking police cars. They saw no survivors and no infected. Once, Gyles thought he saw a man standing in the shade of a tree, but the figure didn't move. If he was human, he didn't want help. The MRAP suddenly stopped at the top of a hill. They were on a dirt road with wide yellow fields of prairie grass on both sides. On the horizon was the outline of a small town.

"You see something?" Gyles asked.

"No, gotta take a piss and get the cramps out," Luke said. He turned back in his seat and said toward the turret. "How we looking out there?"

"All clear," Culver shouted back.

Luke clunked his door open and stepped out into the daylight. Gyles pursed his lips and looked back into the crew compartment. "Let's take ten here, boys." He undid his harness and opened his own door, dropping outside. The air was hot and humid, but it felt good having left the eight-man fart box he was riding in. He moved out away from the vehicle, looking into the field. There was a wire fence just off the shoulder of the road, and beyond that the field stretched out over a hundred yards before ending at a tree line.

Gyles tactically walked up the road and used the optics on his rifle to survey the town ahead. It was typical of others they'd passed. Several small homes on a narrow street. Luke had told him this was the outskirts of a larger city to the north of them. He also said there was a canine training center nearby, that he'd dropped a friend off a couple years ago. Gyles wondered if the place would be populated today.

Fences and heavy walls like a kennel should be secure enough.

He shook his head, not wanting to get distracted. He looked again toward the community ahead. It wasn't a town after all, just a subdivision, a planned housing area like thousands of others that ringed cities across America. To his surprise, he spotted a man walking along the road, moving toward them. The man didn't stagger; he stepped solidly, one foot in front of the other, like he was on an afternoon stroll.

"Contact," Culver shouted. "Twelve o'clock."

Gyles heard men shuffling and returning to the protection of the armor. Gyles stayed on the optic. The man was clean. He wore a light-blue collared dress shirt, khaki pants, and black shoes. No blood, no rips, no open wounds. "Hold your fire," he called out to the gunner. It wasn't a necessary order; the men knew their goal was to stay quiet on the road trip, and popping off an MK19 would be the exact opposite of that.

The man drew closer and Gyles lowered his rifle. He felt someone move behind him, and he turned his head to see Luke standing beside him.

"He's infected, you know," Luke said.

Gyles turned to him. "How do you know?"

"Too mechanical. He's not thinking. He's got a slight limp, but his expression is unchanged, no pain. No discomfort wearing a long-sleeve shirt and walking a blacktop road in the hot Virginia sun."

"You see all that?" Gyles said, impressed at the observation.

"I'm a scout; I have to see those things or get popped."

The man was within a hundred yards now. His pace had changed; he was moving faster and his head began to shift side to side. Luke turned and quickly walked back to the cab of the MRAP. Gyles looked for a bit longer then turned to follow. Inside the MRAP, the engine fired up and the big vehicle pulled forward. Luke cut into the far lane and drove around the infected man. As they passed, Gyles considered the crazed man's eyes. They were glassy and dead inside. He saw no reason in them, no will to live. In the side mirror, Gyles watched as the man turned and began to follow them back down the hill.

"Maybe we should have put him down," Gyles whispered.

Luke shook his head. "It's not worth the time or ammo."

Closer to the subdivision, the housing area lost the appeal it had from the top of the hill. Bodies littered well-manicured lawns. There wasn't a home that didn't have the front windows smashed. Cars were in driveways. Some with luggage on the ground next to them. Doors were open. The community reminded Gyles of those stories where an alarm went off and people raced to get away before a tornado struck.

"Probably caught in the dark. The horde moved over this place like a tsunami," Luke said. "Nobody had a chance."

"Where are they now?" Gyles asked. "Where did the infected go?"

Luke shrugged, keeping his eyes forward as he drove past the remaining homes, increasing his speed to create distance on the place. "I bet the wave doesn't stop. Like the Doc said, these things want to infect everything before cooling down. They probably washed over this spot in no time flat, then continued north to the bigger cities."

The driver slowed again and took them back east onto a hardtop two-lane highway—Virginia State Route 55, according to the sign next to the road. There were more cars now, many disabled in the road. Luke was having to slow often and leave the roadway to go around them.

Gyles sat up in his seat to get a better view. There were guardrails on the left and right, locking them in. He looked at Luke. "We could get stuck in here; you sure this is the route we want?"

Luke stared across at him for a moment with a look that said, *Are you fucking serious?* before lifting his chin toward the trees next to the highway. Taking the man's hint, Gyles focused his attention further out; through the trees on either side of the highway and to the north, he could see the interstate. It was completely blocked. He looked closer and could see craters and destroyed vehicles, signs that the Airforce had put in some work here.

Eventually, the road they were on veered south before going north again, this time passing over the interstate, giving them an up-close look at the destruction. There was no spot on the interstate below that death hadn't touched. Gyles shuddered and shook his head. "Nobody could have survived this."

Luke sighed and took them off the overpass, away from the devastation.

As before, the road ahead was covered in trees, only passing the occasional home or small, one-stop-light town. Gyles looked at his watch and looked up at the sun. In broad daylight they'd only seen a few of the infected. The doctor was, once again, right about their nocturnal nature. Just as Gyles was thinking they were going to have an easy day, Luke slowed and eased the vehicle to the center of the road then stopped.

Ahead of them, the road was blocked. A large gravel hauling trailer was on its side, and just behind that, a pair of police cars parked in a V shape. Gyles leaned forward then looked behind him at Culver, who was already turning in the turret, searching for targets. "What do you see, Culver?"

A roadblock could mean plenty of things. In the old world it would have meant ambush; in this world, possibly nothing more than a massive crime scene. Either way, Gyles didn't want to dismount his men unless he had to.

"I don't see nothing," Culver called out.

Luke looked at Gyles. "It's getting late in the day; we need to keep moving or find a hide. I don't like it, but we can't go back—this is the cleanest route."

Gyles nodded, and Luke put the truck back into

gear, letting it slowly roll forward. Within fifty yards of the overturned trailer, he stopped again. The gravel trailer hadn't flipped; they could tell it was intentionally turned on its side to block the road. The frame of the trailer and wheels pointed back at them, with mounds of dirt covering each end. The police cars were destroyed but not from bullets. The cars were dented in, and every piece of glass was shattered.

"I'm going to get out and see if there is a way around the road block," Gyles said, looking at Luke.

With his eyes locked on the roadblock dead ahead of them, Luke nodded. "Watch your cornhole out there." He then cut the engine, leaving an overwhelming silence as they continued to survey the scene.

Gyles looked back again. "Culver, I'm going out there; anything comes after me, don't blow me up, okay?"

"You got it, boss," the soldier sounded off.

With his grip on the door, Gyles released the combat lock then pushed out just enough that he could exit and drop down to the ground. As his foot hit the road, he heard the clinking of spent brass. Gyles surveyed the ground—9mm and 5.56 brass was scattered everywhere. He froze and turned out, scanning his close surroundings before looking back into the cab. "Someone had a hell of a fight here, expended a lot of rounds."

Luke nodded. "Just see if I can squeeze around that barrier."

Gyles exhaled slowly and took two crouching steps off the roadway and into the grass on the shoulder of the road. The terrain ran up slightly away from him, where it bumped into a tall chain link fence. The far side of the fence was lined with tall trees and thick brush, impossible to see through. He looked at it and shook his head; it would be tough to get across that bramble without being heard. Gyles raised his rifle to the low ready and stealthily moved to the front of the MRAP, stepping heel to toe. He gritted his teeth when he again kicked brass and heard it clinking along the asphalt.

Turning his head, Gyles looked up at Culver. The soldier was dropped down in the turret like a turtle with only the top of his Kevlar and dark-tinted goggles showing. Gyles considered going back. They had plenty of fuel—Luke could find another route. How hard could it be? Clearing his mind of doubts, Gyles halted and took a knee to check his near and far surroundings. He waited, straining for sounds of anything approaching, ensuring nothing had heard the MRAP. Drops of sweat ran down his forehead and into his eyes. He blinked away the sting as he watched a line of ants work their way across the road in front of him. They marched on like nothing was wrong, like it was a regular day and the world wasn't burning. He gritted his teeth and stood, again pulling the rifle into the pocket of his shoulder as he paced forward.

The police cars were directly to his front, parked with their backs to the trailer, the windshields facing him. He sidestepped to the right with his rifle up to clear the cars one at a time. Standing tall, Gyles moved just feet in front of the first vehicle's hood. The windshield was broken, the glue holding it together pulled out. He could tell by the bloody ring surrounding the hole that someone was dragged through it. With a shiver, he stepped around the side. The driver's window still in place, but the outside of the car was streaked with blood. He stopped and searched the ground. *Where the hell are the bodies?*

Gyles turned again to face the trailer. To the right of it was a high dirt berm. A foot path had been pounded into the dirt mound, leading to the top. Although his inner voice screamed at him to turn around and go back to the MRAP, he forced it away and took steps forward until he was just inches from the trailer. He held his breath and listened. Complete silence. Only his breathing and heartbeat filled his ears. He moved to the right and faced the berm before placing a boot on its surface. It was more solid and hardpacked than he'd imagined. Looking back at the MRAP, he could just make out Luke's face. Culver, standing over the MK19 in the turret, flashed him a peace sign.

"Fuck you," he mouthed back, flipping the kid the bird. Gyles moved to the berm and committed to climbing it. Less than ten feet tall and with a low angle, he climbed it easily and was soon at the top. He stepped back and gasped, bile filling his throat. He was at the back of the roadblock, not the front. This was barrier designed to stop traffic from the east, to hold back those fleeing the Capital. Not people like him driving toward it. The roadway ahead was covered with the dead. Unlike the freeways and interstates pounded by the Airforce. The death and decay in front of him was the work of the infected. The smell and heat suddenly hit him in the face.

No longer able to hold it back, he stumbled forward and dropped to his knees, releasing the contents of his stomach. He clawed at the ground and raised his head again, gagging and eyes watering. He cursed himself and dropped to his ass, letting his legs stick out straight. The road went on to the horizon, the entire length filled with destruction and death. Buzzards sat on the ground, picking at bodies as the warm breeze rolled the stench toward him. "And this is the fucking cleanest route," he snarled in a muffled voice.

He heard a clank behind him and turned back to the MRAP. Luke had his door open, checking to see if he was okay. Gyles waved him to go back then forced himself to his feet and wrapped a shemagh around his mouth. On the other side of the berm, there was another set of police cars. Near the dirt berms, a stack of fifty-gallon drums created another barrier on the corners at each end. Gyles pulled his rifle in tight and moved closer, looking down.

He considered the obstacles; if Luke hugged the corner, he'd make it around the barriers. But with wreckage that stretched countless miles ahead, even if they made it around the barriers, it would be a long haul. He shook his head again; they were committed. They could stick to the sides and make a way through the destruction or find a side road. Gyles turned to the MRAP and waved it ahead, pointing off to the side. The Beast's engine fired up, and after a few seconds it was rolling forward.

Gyles climbed as close to the right side of the berm as he could and drew an imaginary line with his hand, directing the MRAP around the barrier. He stood and held his rifle up, looking out toward the congested road as Luke guided the MRAP. The driver expertly eased onto the shoulder of the road, squeezing between the dirt berm and the fence. He saw Luke's face masked in concentration as he needled the vehicle through the gap like a surgeon.

Suddenly, the engine surged and the rear wheels spun, spitting mud and grass. The ground was too soft. The heavy MRAP began to sink in the grass and listed slightly toward him.

Eager to clear the spot, Luke got on the throttle and surged forward, all six wheels engaged and digging in. The MRAP listed more then settled, but in the correction, Luke oversteered and hit the stack of barrels. They clanged down, the pile spilling over the steel drums, smacking the concrete, bouncing and rolling into the dead below. Gyles turned and looked at Culver. The soldier was shaking his head rapidly to the left and right. Gyles pointed his index finger at him harshly as if to say, "Cut it out."

The drums stopped their concert as they dropped to the ground and settled in the mass of bodies. The diesel engine ticked and hummed beside him. Gyles release his grip and exhaled. He could hear his heart pounding in his chest. Luke revved the engine and yanked the wheel, trying to free the stuck vehicle.

Then they came.

CHAPTER TWENTY-THREE

Near Haymarket, Virginia.

It started with roars. Not like a lion or the howling of a wolf, but the deep and manically enraged, fierce screams that only the violently crazed can develop when faced with death. Death that a person or thing no longer fears, a war cry from a monster with no soul.

Body tense and hands shaking, Gyles turned toward the highway of death. He watched them slowly rise among the smoldering wreckage. They must have been asleep in there the entire time. Or were they just waiting? Did they even have the ability to do that? He went to raise his rifle then saw the futility in the action; there were more of them than he had bullets.

He gasped as the brush and trees shook. There were more of them running at the fences, fighting their way through the tree lines. Bloodied and mangled faces fought through the bramble brush and pressed against the chain link fence.

Finally, he got his wits back and turned to the MRAP. Culver was in the turret, firing. *Thunk, thunk, thunk*—the 40mm grenades arced into the highway. Explosive blasts hit the vehicles on the road, but the things didn't stop. They continued running as frags ripped them apart and tossed their shattered bodies. *Thunk, thunk, thunk*. More explosions. Culver was firing closer; soon they would be inside the arming range.

There was no time for Gyles to navigate the berm and barriers around to the passenger door. He ran and leapt to the roof of the vehicle. He landed just behind the turret, his momentum almost taking him completely over the side. He stumbled and tipped before feeling a tug at the back of his jacket.

"Got ya, Sergeant," Culver shouted. He'd stopped firing and was pulling Gyles close.

Gyles regained his footing and, turning back, pushed Culver down through the hatch then dove in after him, head first. Culver was in his harness seat and they quickly became entangled. Weaver was there fast; he pulled the quick release and both tangled men dropped to the floor. Gyles heard the slamming of the hatch and the impacts of the infected against the vehicle at the same time. Luke pressed the accelerator, gunning the MRAP. The vehicle surged forward, the sides pelted like they were in a hailstorm, and so much screaming and pounding the men couldn't hear each other's yells.

Mega was holding his M240 across his chest, screaming. He wanted the hatch open; he wanted to fight. He stuck the barrel through a firing port in the wall and let loose a long stream of gunfire. The sounds of the weapon in the confined space racked all their brains. Sergeant Tucker grabbed him, pulling his shoulders down, and slamming him back into his seat. "Hold your fire," Tucker shouted over the screams.

The rest of the men were flailing a mix of every emotion—from fear, to rage, to panic—all at the same time. Gyles pulled himself from the tangle and forced his body to the front. Luke was holding the wheel in a white-knuckled grip, screaming back at the mass of infected that was now on the hood, their faces pressed against the windshield. The vehicle rocked side to side, and Gyles fell back into the crew compartment.

"I'm losing traction!" Luke yelled. He cut the wheel toward the roadway.

They felt MRAP crunch and grind against abandoned vehicles on the left side. Luke shouted profanities again and cut the wheel back to the right while gunning the engine. The Beast surged forward then bucked violently. The back end bounced as it caught then lost traction. Luke cursed again and threw up his hands. He balled his hands into tight fists and sat back in the seat, defeated. The infected punched and slapped at the bulletproof windshield until their hands became bloody pulps. Luke opened his eyes again and cut the engine. He flipped a middle finger at the things frantically scratching at the windshield. "Bite me," he said.

"What the hell are you doing?" Gyles yelled over the screams of the infected.

"We're stuck. We ain't going anywhere," Luke grunted. "I'm just making it worse."

Gyles panicked. "No—get on it, Luke—push through this mob. This is a damn C-7 diesel!"

Luke shook his head. "It's not a question of horse-power; the ground is too soft on the shoulder and pushing against these things. The back tires are digging in, the front won't even grab traction now. If we want to be able to recover it, I need to stop now, before it's buried so deep we'll need a wrecker to get it out."

Gyles rocked forward and looked behind him. His men were balled up, their heads in their hands. Weaver was in the seat beside Culver, both looking straight ahead. Culver had his hands over his ears, mumbling to himself, "We can't stay here... we can't stay here... we can't stay here..."

"I'm sorry, Gyles. This thing isn't moving until we can get some traction under those tires."

"We can't go out there," Gyles said.

"Not suggesting we do. Not yet, anyway. But in the morning maybe." He looked in the back. There were six cases of MREs strapped into one of the seats. Luke pointed at them. "Give me that MRE box."

"Seriously? You're hungry now?"

Luke shook his head and rolled his eyes. "I need

the cardboard, dumbass. I want to block up these windows. Maybe if they can't see us they'll forget about us and go away. You know how they act like a fat kid at a buffet—they don't see any more chicken nuggets, they want to go home."

"You think that'll work?"

"I don't know, but if their brains are fried, maybe it will," Luke said, shaking his open hand for the box. "You have a better idea?"

"I don't want to stay the night here."

Luke laughed. "We'll put on footie pajamas and have a campout. Mega can tell ghost stories and we'll swap MREs. It'll be fun. Seriously, hand me that fucking box."

Gyles moved to the back and cut the ties on the top MRE case, pulling it open and dumping the contents onto the floor. He passed the box to the front then opened the next five. He broke down the boxes and returned to the passenger seat. They pressed the cardboard into the widows and used rolls of hundred-mile-an-hour tape, a type of military-grade duct tape, to seal them into the windshield and side windows. The block windows in the rear were still uncovered but so high off the ground, the infected couldn't see in them.

It was still loud outside but not seeing the infected clawing and pounding at the windshield made the noise less terrifying. Gyles looked at the empty passenger seat in the front but showed no interest in moving there. He moved to one of the bucket seats in the troop compartment and fell into it. He pulled off his helmet, surprised it had stayed on his head during the entire ordeal. He looked over the men; they'd calmed down.

The M240 was back on the floor next to Mega's outstretched feet. The big man's head was tilted back, and he was staring up at the ceiling. The rest of the men looked the same—physically and mentally exhausted. The scene reminded Gyles of old World War II movies he watched with his dad as a kid. Worn out and exhausted men in the belly of a submarine, trying to stay quiet so the enemy destroyers above wouldn't hear them and go away. Culver reached for a bottle of water and knocked over his rifle, which clanged to the floor. They were rewarded with fifteen minutes of frenzied activity outside.

"I don't even know why I joined the damn Army," Culver whispered.

Sergeant Tucker sat up and gave the kid a serious stare. "Good thing you did, or your ugly ass would be out there with them, instead of in here."

Mega started to laugh. Tucker turned and shot him a hard finger. "Don't you even open that damn blowhorn of yours."

That was all it took, and Mega was having a fit of laughter that the others joined in on. "I know it's fucked up, but I can't stop," Mega said, holding his belly.

Tucker moved closer and held his hands over the big man's mouth, jokingly. The infected outside banged at the armor, their screams dulled and not as loud as before.

Luke looked back. "Damn ladies. You all do know the basics of what we are trying to do, right? You ever play hide-and-seek as a kid?"

Gyles shook his head and moved back to the bench seat across from Weaver, who reached across the gap and handed him a warm bottle of water. Gyles put it to his mouth and drank half of it, not realizing how thirsty he was until the water hit his lips. His hands were shaking from the adrenaline, and he realized his clothing was soaked with sweat. He set the half-empty bottle beside him and peeled off his uniform top. The other men began doing the same. It was hot outside, and with the engine off, it had to be approaching a hundred degrees inside.

All the interior vents and firing ports were open. There was a slight breeze, but the airflow carried the stench of death and decay, which only made things worse. Weaver looked at him. "How fucked are we?"

"Like a flesh light at football camp," Gyles grunted back.

The crew compartment of men again let out bellows of laughter, only the way soldiers facing death could. Mega's booming voice echoed. The others laughed harder at the absurdity of the big man's obscenely loud voice when all of them were trying to remain quiet.

"Damn ya'll hooting and hollering like a bunch of sorority girls back there," Luke shouted from the front.

That caused only more laughter. Soon they were panted out, breathing hard and sweating. The stink was beginning to stick to them, and they could taste it on their mouths. The men weren't complaining about the heat yet. They'd been in the Iraqi desert less than a month ago, and they still remembered what real heat felt like. They were dressing down and drinking water.

Gyles looked at his watch: nearly 1700 hours. It would be dark in a few hours and the temps would drop some, not much—but the sun off the MRAP would help cool it. The ravaging infected outside had tempered down; what was once feverish slamming against the sides of the vehicle had lulled and slowed to a dull tapping against the windshield.

Moving from his seat to the cupola, Gyles looked up through glass blocks in the bottom and scanned a three-sixty. As Luke had predicted, the infected were already leaving. The things did have a short attention span, but how far would they go? He watched some walk out of view as several others remained close by. A mob of what used to be young men walked through the wreckage, picking over the dead to their front. Others walked the highway, weaving in and out of the abandoned cars. He dropped back down and climbed into the front passenger seat. Luke had his head back; he thought the man was asleep.

"How's it looking out there?" Luke said, the sound of his voice in the silence startling him.

Gyles looked over at the driver then back to the

taped cardboard to his front. "They are thinning out. Maybe you're right, and by morning they'll be gone."

Luke grunted and stretched like he was in his Lazy Boy recliner at home. He seemed content to be stuck on the side of the road, like this was just another day off, and he didn't have shit to do. "When you were out there earlier, you see anything solid we can hook the winch cable to? I reckon we could pull ourselves out if we have to," the man said, leaving his eyes closed and his arms crossed on his chest.

Gyles nodded, thinking about it. "Probably. I guess some of those trees beyond the fence could be beefy enough to do it. Maybe even a fence post. We can't be in that deep." He looked at the radio and pointed. "Any word?"

"Nope. Like a ghost town out there. Nobody. Everything is buzzing. Even the local police nets and trucker traffic is static."

"How far did we get?" Gyles asked. "How much further do we have to go?"

"We're about fifty miles to Belvoir." Luke paused then said, "You know what's bothering me, though, is Mount Weather is just north of here. I thought for sure they would have been broadcasting."

"What the hell is Mount Weather?"

Luke looked at Gyles and shook his head in disappointment. "It's a big shop for FEMA. Not only that... it's sort of a hub for the Emergency Alert System."

"What? Those pops and beeps on the radio?"

Gyles said. "I didn't know that came from a place, just thought it was local thing."

Luke shrugged. "I don't know how it all works, but I know there is a big control center for it up there on the mountain. My cousin was a radio tech in the Navy. After he got out he got a job with them. He told me about all kinds of high-tech shit they had up there."

Gyles pointed at the radio in front of him. Under the big police radio mounted below the window was a traditional AM\FM deck. "What station are they on? Let's see what they have to say."

Luke shook his head again. "It's not like that; they'd be all over the spectrum. Doesn't matter, though. Everything is down."

"Down? What makes you say that?" Gyles asked. "Maybe it's just off. Or we're out of range."

Luke shook his head. "If the religious freaks on the AM dial have gone silent, you know something is wrong. I tried earlier, just a steady buzz on every channel." He sighed and looked at Gyles. "Seriously, bro, you've never heard of Mount Weather?"

Pursing his lips, Gyles shrugged. "I don't know. I remember stuff about a doomsday bunker, but that was just all comic book shit... or maybe something I saw in a movie."

Luke pointed his finger at him and smiled. "See, Sergeant? You ain't as clueless as I thought."

"What, that doomsday bunker shit is real?"

Luke laughed quietly and nodded his head slowly up and down. "Hell, yeah, it's real. My cousin said during 9/11, helicopters were dropping big-time government folks in there around the clock. They didn't come back out until the all-clear was given. Some say Dick Cheney even moved into that crib. Yeah, that shit is real."

"If they are so dug in and sealed up, then why aren't they broadcasting? You think the infection got them?"

Luke sucked in his lips and shrugged. "It's something I was wondering about myself. Even if they were all dead and gone, we should still hear unit traffic, HAM radio operators, some remote radio stations. Hell... just other guys like us stuck in a cab out on the road... you know, shit like that. Do you remember the night this started?"

"How could I forget?" Gyles said. "I had no clue what was about to go down."

"You remember the radios? The cell phones? I was working at the station. There was so much damn traffic, we could hardly get through to the deputies. And state police, after a few beats... forget about it. Everything was jammed up; the nets were useless."

Gyles dipped his chin in agreement. He remembered listening to the chaos from the Chinook.

Luke reached forward and adjusted the volume on the AM\FM radio, turning it down almost all the way. He powered it on and hit scan. The digital dial spun, catching nothing two straight passes through. He pushed a button and manually dialed it to 93.7 then looked at Gyles. "This was a popular station up here.

The Emergency Broadcast System should be pushing messages traffic through it. What do you hear?"

Gyles listened to the steady buzz with its occasional ticks and whirr of static. "It's just buzzing and clicking."

"Listen to the clicks. Weed out all the rest of the noise, ignore the buzzing," Luke said. The man waited, holding his fingers on the volume dial.

Gyles intensified his stare and leaned forward with his eyes closed, concentrating. There was a click then he counted with his fingers. After six seconds there was another click, then another six seconds later, and another six seconds after that. "What is it?" Gyles asked.

"I don't know, but check this out." He flipped the dial over to AM. The same buzz, and at the same six-second interval there were clicks. Then Luke turned off the radio and flipped on the police scanner. The same buzzing and clicking at the same six second interval. Luke turned them all off and sat back in his seat. "Different frequencies, different spectrums, even different radios and antennas. I think Mount Weather is up. That is a loop; it's not by accident."

"Then why aren't they talking?" Gyles asked.

"Because they are jamming us, jamming everything. Most likely everything except short-range and military nets dialed in direct. Probably why you could talk to the colonel at Hunter from the Stryker. But you couldn't hear anyone else. That's just a guess. I don't know shit about radios, other than pushing buttons."

"Why would they jam everything?" Gyles said, doubtful. "What's the point of taking down communications so people can't be warned? Why keep us from talking?"

"Hey—they sent all those messages on TV and the radio early on, told folks to stay put, and it didn't work. If people had locked up like they were told, the police and military could have done their jobs. The infection never would have spread to places like Vines. It never would have crossed state lines." Luke paused and took a deep breath. "They took it down because the network news started talking about safe areas and FEMA camps in places like Atlanta. I think they turned all that shit off to keep people from moving around, stop folks from spreading the virus."

Luke looked hard at Gyles. "They wanted to stop shit like that guy telling everyone to go west to Fort Knox. Telling people to get the hell out of the Capital. Keep people off the roads." Luke swallowed hard and pointed at the sky. "Maybe even to keep that shit about bombing highways and culling survivors quiet."

Gyles sighed. "That's a hell of an idea. Doctor Howard actually said something about the only hope to really stop and contain the virus was for people to stay home. To stop spreading it."

"You know it's true. It has to be what's going on," Luke said. "Not like we don't have a precedent for jamming communications when we fight an enemy. Like Howard said, people are the infection, they want to stop them from moving. News about FEMA camps and safe areas give people hope. It gets them out on the road."

Gyles went to speak when they heard the roaring of the infected outside. They were screaming, but they weren't pounding on the MRAP; the sounds were moving away from them. Then suddenly the screams were joined with the noise of a loud diesel engine. Gyles looked at Luke, who reached to his front and peeled back a bit of the MRE cardboard. A bright light shone in at them. Gyles squinted and considered the beams. Something big and loud was moving directly at them. "What the hell is it?"

CHAPTER TWENTY-FOUR

DAY OF INFECTION PLUS ELEVEN, 2100 HOURS

Near Haymarket, Virginia.

"Who the hell are they?" Luke said, pulling the rest of the cardboard off the windshield. "And what do they want?"

Gyles held a hand over his eyes, blocking the bright spotlights. "I don't know what they are, but they've got the infected pissed off. So, I'm on their side."

The vehicle moved closer, the intense beams no longer directed at them, but over and to the sides. The vehicle was big and yellow, scorched with burn marks and splattered with blood. It groaned and grunted, belching clouds of black smoke. A large spike-toothed bucket extended out toward them. Gyles flinched back, waiting for it to crash through the cab of the MRAP. Instead, it dropped down and clenched the front of the vehicle with a screech of metal-on-metal. The front end of the 30,000-pound armored vehicle shuddered and rose off the ground. They shook back and forth as the MRAP settled onto the hook.

"Aww shit, here's to hoping they are the good guys," Luke said, lifting his hands off the wheel.

The yellow vehicle to the front groaned, and the bright spotlights on the back of the vehicle powered off as others turned on in the opposite direction. Luke strained forward, keeping his hands off the wheel as they were dragged ahead, along the side of the road. "It's a bulldozer, a big-as-shit bulldozer."

Gyles looked ahead and could see the big CAT symbol on the back of the oversized machine. A cab centered on the top was covered in welded-on plate steel. Infected were all over the dozer. Occasional muzzle flashes from inside the cab knocked them off when they managed to get too tight a grip onto the steel grating. In the crew compartment, the soldiers had their faces pressed against the side windows, observing the chaos and infected horde outside.

"I don't care who they are, they are getting us the hell off this road," Mega shouted. "You see all these things out here, Sergeant?"

Gyles shifted. The side of the road was once again packed with them. The creatures were back in force. If they'd attempted to dig out of the vehicle the next morning, they would have certainly been killed. He looked back to the front as the dozer slowed. They were leaving the highway. A mile from where they'd been stranded at the roadblock, the dozer made a hard turn.

The MRAP bucked and protested, the metal screeching as it was dragged around a hard corner. They were now moving on an elevated road about twenty feet wide, the infected still packed in around them. Ahead, they could see steel walls and bright lights shining down. Muzzle flashes popped like strobes all along the perimeter of the building. There was a gate ahead and just outside of it, the dozer stopped and the bucket lowered fast, slamming the MRAP back to the surface with a steel-crunching thud and the suspension protested.

The dozer moved ahead and turned right down a steep decline, leaving. At the bottom, the dozer again made a sharp turn through sections of dragon's teeth barriers laid out on a narrow path below. Cutting right and into cover, its lights were suddenly shut off and the dozer vanished from view as it continued a trek with most of the creatures still in pursuit.

Gyles sat, stunned. The building ahead of them was massive—concrete walls the first eight feet, then plate steel over that. Outside the walls was a large span of blacktop then a high steel fence that completely enclosed the structure. Surrounding the outside of the fence, ten to twelve deep, were the infected.

Before Gyles could ask how they were going to deal with the crazies outside, the perimeter lights of the compound shut off. The firing stopped. Gyles lost sight of the building in the darkness. He reached for his night vision goggles, but before he could find them, there was a faraway explosion—a ball of fire that lit up the night sky.

The infected along the fence pulled away and stared directly into the distant inferno. A building maybe a quarter mile from them was in flames. The crazies were consumed with it. Screaming and howling, they turned and ran toward the fire. Gyles looked across at Luke. The man shook his head then pointed toward a gate. A man in Marine Corps camo was standing just beyond it. He pointed up, and they spotted a small tower they hadn't seen before. A man was frantically waving them forward. Luke hit the ignition, firing up the engine. He put the MRAP in gear and edged forward. Just before they hit the gate, it slid to the left. The Marine on the ground guided them in then ordered the gate closed behind them. The man outside walked in front of the MRAP and, with a red flashlight, directed them with hand signals, waving them ahead. Luke followed his instructions. A large bay door opened in the side of the steel building.

They followed the ground guide into a large concrete bay filled with other military vehicles. The Marine on the ground turned around and pointed at the cab of the MRAP and ran a slicing motion across his throat. Luke reached down and killed the engine. The Marine flashed a thumbs up then walked away. In the silence, they could hear the bay doors closing behind them then a trio of men in uniform moved in their direction from the right.

"What the hell just happened?" Gyles mumbled.

"Bout to find out," Luke said. He unlatched his door and dropped outside. The Marine who had been guiding them turned back and raised his rifle, seemingly surprised that the driver would exit without instruction. Luke's hands shot into the air.

"Aw, hell," Gyles said. He opened his own door and dropped to the ground. More rifles were turned on him from Marines to his side he hadn't seen before.

"On your knees," the Marines barked.

Gyles held his hands up and dropped to a knee. "Calm down, hero. I ain't a bad guy," he said, his head swiveling. "Name's Sergeant First Class Robert Gyles. Just trying to link back up with my command at Fort Belvoir."

"Slow it down, Devil Dogs," a stern voice barked from the trio.

Gyles's head drifted back toward the trio. A silver-haired man with a strong jaw walked directly toward them. He wore black eagles on his collars and the name McDuffie on his shirt. He moved just to the front of the vehicle and eyed Luke, then turned to Gyles. "Got me a cop and a busted-up soldier riding in a painted-over MRAP." A door slammed behind them and a crew of men stomped in, one wearing olive-green coveralls and a pistol in a shoulder holster. The colonel looked to the group. "Any problems out there?"

The guy in the coveralls shook his head no. "In and out, sir. We're secure, but these fools were stuck good out there. They never would have gotten out on their own."

"That's debatable," Luke said.

The man obviously in charge smiled at the comment then turned back to the front. "So, what were you ladies doing out joy riding on my road? You shook things up this afternoon, probably drew another ten thousand infected into the area with that shit show you all put on."

Luke went to speak, but the colonel held up his hand and pointed at Gyles. "Let the sergeant talk."

Gyles cleared his throat. "We are trying link up with what's left of my unit back in Fort Belvoir—Sir."

The colonel slowly shook his head side to side. "Now, what wild hair did you get on your ass to make you think it was a promising idea to go to Belvoir? Belvoir is a damned nightmare, son. Not a damn person left alive there. We been risking blood and treasure to get folks out, yet you want to go in."

Gyles's chin dropped, the air sucking from his chest, and he let out a long breath. "Sa..." he paused and looked down at the ground. "Sir, I—we—are trying to link up with my division, sir."

"You were with the Third?" McDuffie softened his tone.

"I *am* with the Third," Gyles corrected, his eyes still down. "My company is still there. Captain Younger is my commanding officer."

McDuffie sighed, his face softening. "Get on your feet, soldier, and put your damn hands down." Gyles stood and McDuffie moved closer, extending his hand. "I'm Colonel Glen McDuffie. This is what's left of my Combat Engineer Battalion. We've got some Seabees held up here too."

"You're all Engineers?" Gyles asked.

The colonel nodded his head yes. "You got wounded in there, any infected, signs of infection?"

Gyles shook his head no. "No, sir, just what's left of my platoon. We're not infected."

McDuffie turned to a man next to him. "Get those troops out of there. Get 'em fed and cleaned up. Make sure the Doc gives them all a good inspection then put them to bed." The young Marine ran off toward the MRAP and climbed up into Gyles's passenger door. Soon after, there was an electronic hum as the back hatch dropped down. McDuffie pointed to Luke and waved him closer. "Listen, I am going to need a full debrief from you two." Luke began to speak and McDuffie raised his hand. "Not now. I would like to have my S2 present, if you are up for it."

"Can do, sir," Gyles said. Luke stood by his side, not speaking, but McDuffie caught a glimpse of his scoped, crossed-rifles tattoo with the word *Scout* written under it.

The colonel stopped and rubbed the stubble on his chin, staring at Luke's neck. "You a Marine, son? Or do you just use that tattoo to chase tail?"

Luke bit at his bottom lip and nodded. "Yes, sir. A Marine. I got out of the Corps in 2003."

"Hmm, you got out, you say. Well... we'll see about

that." He turned back to a young officer standing behind him. "Lieutenant, get these men some chow." He stopped and looked them over again, wrinkling his nose. "Yeah, a shower and a change of clothes too. Then bring them upstairs to the conference room."

CHAPTER TWENTY-FIVE

DAY OF INFECTION PLUS TWELVE, 0100 HOURS

Near Haymarket, Virginia.

They say that war never sleeps, and Gyles was finding that out the hard way as he was led down a long corridor. He showered and shaved, dressed in a clean uniform—a hand-me-down set of Marine Corps MARPAT (Marine Pattern) with the name tapes and patches removed. But there was no reason to bitch when the trousers and blouse weren't covered in gore and grime, and his hair was no longer crusted with dried blood and dirt. He walked slowly, feeling the exertion of every step. He really was tired.

The hall opened to a large factory floor, where Marines and Seabees were sitting on the edges of evenly spaced cots. Some were at tables, cleaning weapons, while others just slept. There was a galley line where men with trays grabbed sandwiches from a table. In another corner was a space that looked like a medical triage center. "How many you got here?" Gyles asked the young officer escorting them.

"Over five hundred when it's all added up. We have other buildings too. This is just the active part of the camp." The Marine turned and pointed. At the end of the floor were stairs that led up to a mezzanine with glassed-in offices. The officer stepped ahead of them and opened a door to a conference room. Gyles felt the cool air conditioning immediately, and his body tingled at the sensation. He took two steps in and saw McDuffie standing over a large map overlay.

To his right was a blonde-haired major. Tall and lanky, his face was gaunt with dark shadows under his eyes. At the back of the room, leaning against a whiteboard, holding a coffee cup was a leathered senior enlisted man. The old man was stocky, his hair shaved down to nothing. If Gyles had to bet, he'd guess the man both cut his hair and shaved with a K-Bar. He looked like he could wrestle a bear and win. As soon as the man saw Luke and Gyles, he locked cold eyes on them.

McDuffie ordered the pair into the room and sat them around a large conference table that took up the majority of the free space. On a back wall was a sofa with an olive sleeping bag laid out on it. Duffel bags of gear leaned in every corner with a pair of cots on an opposite wall. The colonel made quick introductions. The S2 officer was Major Dale Mabry. He was an intelligence officer in name only. His specialty was in Operations and Security. The other man was Master

Gunnery Sergeant Allen "Gus" Gustafson, the current senior enlisted leader for the battalion.

At the end of the conference table was a tray with a coffee pot and foam cups. Parts of MREs were laid out, and someone had raided a vending machine of sweet and salty snacks. McDuffie pointed at the cups, and Gyles nodded, reaching for one and topping it off before handing the pot to Luke. "So where exactly is it you are coming from, Sergeant Gyles?" McDuffie asked.

Gyles blew on the surface of the coffee and took in a sip. "I'm with Second Platoon, India Company—"

McDuffie interrupted. "Yeah, I get all of that; you're with the Third out of Fort Stewart. But how did you get out there, when your battalion is up at the grinder?" the colonel said, pointing toward the road.

"The grinder, sir?"

McDuffie frowned and dipped his chin. "The Meat Grinder; it's what the battle for the Capital is being called... for obvious reasons."

"Yes, sir. I understand," Gyles said, looking down.

Mabry cleared his throat and reached back for the large map and slid it to their front. They had the location of the manufacturing plant they were currently in circled in red grease marker. The road they had been traveling on was marked over heavy in black.

Gyles nodded and started his story over. He told them about the mission to the laboratory in Northern Virginia, how the mission had failed and they retreated to Vines when Hunter Field waved them off from their return leg. He told them about the armory, how it was overrun and they fled with the surviving civilians into the national forest. The information they received from Colonel Erickson at the roadblock and the details on Fort Stewart. Then finally, he talked about the civilians who wandered into their camp just the night before. When Gyles finished, he looked at Luke. "Anything you want to add?"

Luke shook his head no. Mabry looked at the notes he'd been taking the entire time Gyles was speaking. "You say you had a CH-47. Where is it now?"

Gyles nodded. "Yes, sir; we had one. It departed this morning. We lost contact with it when it went to a civilian airfield, looking for fuel. They either made it and continued on to Stewart or they are still out there somewhere."

"And you had more with you? National Guard, police and civilians? You sent them on to Fort Knox in Kentucky?"

"Yes, sir."

McDuffie nodded. "That was a smart move. As far as we can tell, infection is lighter on that side of the Appalachians. If they stuck to it, they should have arrived okay. I don't know why in the hell you boys would travel east. You should have stayed with those people and went with them."

"I told you, we heard our company is—" Gyles looked at the map. "Our company was at Fort Belvoir, we needed to—"

The old Master Gunner Sergeant slammed a hand

against the desk. "If they were at the damned Meat Grinder, those poor bastards are either dead or walking around infected. Just get them out of your head; the sooner the better."

"Understood," Gyles said, locking his eyes on the older man, pretending not to be intimidated.

"I don't think you do, son. I don't think you understand the severity of the Meat Grinder."

Gus looked back at Gyles with a thousand-yard stare, like he was looking through him, his hard jaw set. "The President had a novel idea to send every swinging dick to defend the Capital. All we did was feed the infected army. For every ten we sent, seven would become infected. Those men turned on us, some of them back in aid centers. We didn't have a chance. The more we lost, the more troops they sent in. On top of that, all the fighting, bombing... the fires... all of it drew everything in—every infected person for a hundred miles converged on the Capital. My scouts have killed crazies out there with Florida driver's licenses. You know how many damn people were between here and Florida?"

Gyles looked at Luke then back to the Master Gunnery Sergeant. "I—I don't know."

"A fucking lot, that's how many." The man snarled. "A lot."

McDuffie raised his hands. "All right, Gus, put the wagons back in the barn. These boys have seen their fair share. I think they get it."

"So then..." Gyles paused.

"What are we doing out here?" McDuffie finished the thought.

"Yeah, this isn't a base. It looks like an old factory."

McDuffie smiled and pointed to Mabry, who nodded his head and said, "We're combat engineers. Once the task force realized what was happening, that the fighting in the Capital was more than dealing with protestors and it was just drawing in more infected, we were deployed out of Camp Lejeune. They called us up to build barriers and to create choke points to delay the enemy advance. We linked up with a bunch of Seabees out of Little Creek, Virginia, in Richmond. At first our mission was fairly basic... laying wire, building sandbag walls and towers for units defending the Capital. But once the Pentagon fell we were—"

"The Pentagon fell?" Gyles said.

"Yes, on day nine." Mabry continued. "The Pentagon, Capital Building, the Whitehouse... it all fell together, and after that we were pushed out of the city. Our battalion was ordered to blow all the major bridges and overpasses to block the flow of infected in or out. Those orders were short-lived when the combat outposts ringing the city started getting overrun and the Airforce started dropping everything they had on the hordes. We were then instructed to find shelter and ordered to dig in and get hard.

"We took positions just outside the city where two major interstates crossed. Built walls, barriers, trenches. Hell, we planted explosives and had claymores around us on all sides. Even with all of that, we held for twenty-four hours. They came and came at us until we were buttoned up on our armored vehicles and heavy equipment. We tried to bug out, but with the highways like this and the constant attacks from the infected, we didn't make it very far.

"Once we lost contact from command and orders for air support, we decided on the mountains. Original plan was to get to the national forest, same as you. Just didn't have the fuel for it. Sure, there are loads of civilian gas stations and tanker trucks, but that's some uphill sledding to recover fuel while fighting off the infected. Eventually our scouts found this spot and we could reasonably secure it, so we took up residence.

"The foundations of the buildings are poured concrete. The walls sheet steel. Best of all, the place was already equipped with some solar lighting and backup generators. All we had to do is reinforce the fencing and build that raised approach road so the infected couldn't swamp our vehicles when we came and went. Since then it's been nothing but making it stronger and hoping we can find survivors."

"Have you?" Gyles asked. "Are you finding survivors?"

McDuffie spoke up. "We've been monitoring radio traffic, trying to run patrols when we can. We send drones up and down the interstate three times a day. We find civilians not infected, we take them in. That's how we spotted you all out there on Route 55. Watched you put on that fireworks show and get yourselves stuck."

"And you are sure D.C. is a loss?" Gyles asked.

McDuffie turned to his operations officer. Mabry nodded. "I have drone footage of the last troops bailing out of Belvoir and Quantico. Solid information that most of the units rolled north, civilians and officers being flown out as the Capital fell. We lost communications with everyone just a couple days ago. Drones are only spotting infected on the ground. There is nothing there worth going to, and nobody is talking."

"We think someone is jamming the airwaves," Luke said, speaking for the first time.

Mabry nodded. "Yes, our communications people suspect the same thing. I've seen it done personally in Syria during air raids, so it's not out of the question that they wouldn't be doing it now. Radios are behaving the same way as what I remember. The gear is working, but outside of a few hundred yards, we just get buzzing. The buzzing started right after the Airforce kicked off Operation Hecatomb."

"Hecatomb—that's the bombing," Gyles said. "They killed a lot of innocent people."

Mabry set his jaw and shook his head. "So did the infected; they did what they had to. It's not easy to keep your hands clean in this fight, Sergeant."

"Fuck that," Luke said. He shook his head and looked back down at the map. "I never put on a uniform to kill civilians."

Gus laughed from the other side of the table. The two looked at each other until finally Luke said, "So, what's next? What exactly do we have going on here?"

Gus laughed again, more maniacal than the last time. He leaned in and locked eyes with Luke. "We keep digging in and stay alive. We send out patrols when we can and bring people back when we find them. We have two hundred Marines and almost as many Seabees in this compound. In a building next door there are almost seven hundred civilians. Of those civilians, a third can carry a rifle. As soon as we have enough gear, ammo, and men, we are going to bring them the fight."

"The fight?" Gyles asked

"This war isn't over, and if you think it is, then you better wipe yourself off and harden up, soldier. What you are looking at here is the Alamo, and we are about to change history—this Alamo isn't going to fall." Gus raised his voice and slammed his hand on the table again. "We are at war. And this ain't over until we kill every damn one of them!"

THANK YOU FOR READING

Please leave a review on Amazon.
About WJ Lundy

W. J. Lundy is a still serving Veteran of the U.S. Military with service in Afghanistan. He has over 16 years of combined service with the Army and Navy in Europe, the Balkans and Southwest Asia. W.J. is an avid athlete, writer, backpacker and shooting enthusiast. He currently resides with his wife and daughter in Central Michigan.

Find WJ Lundy on Facebook:
Join the WJ Lundy mailing list for news, updates and contest giveaways.

GET IT HERE

Whiskey Tango Foxtrot is an introduction into the apocalyptic world of Staff Sergeant Brad Thompson. A series with over 1,500 five-star reviews on Amazon.

Alone in a foreign land. The radio goes quiet while on convoy in Afghanistan, a lost patrol alone in the desert. With his unit and his home base destroyed, Staff Sergeant Brad Thompson suddenly finds himself isolated and in command of a small group of men trying to survive in the Afghan wasteland.

Every turn leads to danger. The local population has been afflicted with an illness that turns them into rabid animals. They pursue him and his men at every corner and stop. Struggling to hold his team together and unite survivors, he must fight and evade his way to safety.

A fast paced zombie war story like no other.

Escaping The Dead
    Tales of The Forgotten
    Only The Dead Live Forever
    Walking In The Shadow Of Death
    Something To Fight For
    Divided We Fall
    Bound By Honor
    Primal Resurrection

Praise for Whiskey Tango Foxtrot:

"The beginning of a fantastic story. Action packed and full of likeable characters. If you want military authenticity, look no further. You won't be sorry."

-Owen Baillie, Author of Best-selling series, Invasion of the Dead.

"A brilliantly entertaining post-apocalyptic thriller. You'll find it hard to putdown"

-Darren Wearmouth, Best-selling author of First Activation, Critical Dawn, Sixth Cycle

"W.J. Lundy captured two things I love in one novel--military and zombies!"

-Terri King, Editor Death Throes Webzine

"War is horror and having a horror set during wartime works well in this story. Highly recommended!"

-Allen Gamboa, Author of Dead Island: Operation Zulu

"There are good books in this genre, and then there are the ones that stand out from the rest-- the ones that make me want to purchase all the books in the series in one shot and keep reading. W.J. Lundy's Whiskey Tango Foxtrot falls into the latter category."

-Under the Oaks reviews

"The author's unique skills set this one apart from the masses of other zombie novels making it one of the most exciting that I have read so far."

-HJ Harry, of Author Splinter

THE INVASION TRILOGY

GET IT HERE

The Darkness is a fast-paced story of survival that brings the apocalypse to Main Street USA.

While the world falls apart, Jacob Anderson barricades his family behind locked doors. News reports tell of civil unrest in the streets, murders, and disappearances; citizens are warned to remain behind locked doors. When Jacob becomes witness to horrible events and the alarming actions of his neighbors, he and his family realize everything is far worse than being reported.

Every father's nightmare comes true as Jacob's normal life--and a promise to protect his family--is torn apart.

From the Best-Selling Author of **Whiskey Tango Foxtrot comes a new telling of Armageddon.**

The Darkness

The Shadows

The Light

Praise for the Invasion Trilogy:

"The Darkness is like an air raid siren that won't shut off; thrilling and downright horrifying!" *Nicholas Sansbury Smith, Best Selling Author of Orbs and The Extinction Cycle.*

"Absolutely amazing. This story hooked me from the first page and didn't let up. I read the story in one sitting and now I am desperate for more. ...Mr. Lundy has definitely broken new ground with this tale of humanity, sacrifice and love of family ... In short, read this book." *William Allen, Author of Walking in the Rain.*

"First book I've pre-ordered before it was published. Well done story of survival with a relentless pace, great action, and characters I cared about! Some scenes are still in my head!" *Stephen A. North, Author of Dead Tide and The Drifter.*

DONOVAN'S WAR

GET IT HERE

The Author of the bestselling series _Whiskey Tango Foxtrot,_ returns with Tommy Donovan, on a war path of destruction to save the only family he has left.

With everything around him gone. Tommy Donovan must return to the war he has been hiding from. When his sister is taken, the Government fails to act. Tommy Donovan will take the law into his own hands. But, this time he isn't a soldier, and there will be no laws to protect evil. This time it's personal and he is making the rules.

Resigned to never finding peace from the war long behind him, retired warrior, Thomas Donovan, is now faced with an even deadlier conflict... one that could cost him the last of his humanity.

Once a member of an elite underground unit, the only wars Thomas knows now are the ones that rage inside him. All he wants is to stay under the radar of existence, trying to forget the past and isolating himself from the present.

When extremists kidnap a group of women from a Christian church in Syria, the past and present collide,forcing Donovan to act. This time, the battle is personal. This time, evil has chosen the wrong victim, and Thomas Donovan will not stop until he has made those responsible pay.

Facing insurmountable odds in hostile territories and always one step behind, will he be too late to save the life of the one he holds dear?

"Riveting unexpected twists, gritty realism, and first-hand adventure are inside this book. Get it now." - JL Bourne, author of Tomorrow War and Day by Day Armageddon.

"Donovan's War is an intense, non-stop thriller that begins with just enough of the main character's back-story to make you want to keep reading, without getting you bogged down with page after page of info dump to establish that Tommy is a world-class bad ass." Brian Parker, author of A Path of Ashes.

They took Tommy's Sister ...and you don't mess with Tommy's family.

OTHER BOOKS FROM UNDER THE
SHIELD OF

FIVE ROADS TO TEXAS

| LUNDY | GAMBOA | HANSEN | BAKER | PARKER |

From the best story tellers of Phalanx Press comes a frightening tale of Armageddon.

It spread fast- no time to understand it- let alone learn how to fight it.

Once it reached you, it was too late. All you could do is run.

Rumored safe zones and potential for a cure drifted across the populace, forcing tough decisions to be made.

They say only the strong survive. Well they forgot about the smart, the inventive and the lucky.

Follow five different groups from across the U.S.A. as they make their way to what could be America's last stand in the Lone Star State.

GET IT NOW ON AMAZON

AFTER THE ROADS

BRIAN PARKER

The infected rule the world beyond the protective walls of the Texas Safe Zone.

Fort Bliss, Texas is home to four million refugees, trapped behind the hastily-erected walls of the Army base--too many people and not enough food.

In a desperate gamble, the soldiers responsible for securing the walls begin searching for pre-outbreak food storage locations. Not everyone will make it home.

For Sidney Bannister, the Safe Zone's refugee camps have become a nightmare that she can no longer endure. She must find a way to leave before her baby is born, or risk never experiencing freedom again.

Follow Sidney's story from the Phalanx Press collaborative novel Five Roads to Texas.

FOR WHICH WE STAND

JOSEPH HANSEN

El Paso wasn't the Promised Land that Ian and his crew had hoped for but it wasn't a total bust either. The concept of a safe haven in today's world was a fool's errand at best. This was the consensus of their tiny band and to keep moving, their only salvation. While others waited in their pens the four from the private security company moved on taking on as many they could help, in hopes that they too would join the fight. Their journey was long and arduous but it was worth it... they hope.

El Paso is where the final evidence that this is more than a simple lab experiment gone wrong. It was too focused with too many players who knew too much too early in the game causing assumptions to be made. Assumptions that gained strength with every step they took until the small troop was convinced that this was not just a simple virus of natural origins, America was under attack.

For Which We Stand is a post-apocalyptic thriller that lends credence to the fears that many share. Is it possible? No one can say, Five Roads to Texas is but one of hundreds end of the world scenarios. We all know it's coming, how and when is the only question.

SIXTH CYCLE

CARL SINCLAIR & DARREN WEARMOUTH

Nuclear war has destroyed human civilization.

Captain Jake Phillips wakes into a dangerous new world, where he finds the remaining fragments of the population living in a series of strongholds, connected across the country. Uneasy alliances have maintained their safety, but things are about to change. --

Discovery **leads to danger.** -- Skye Reed, a tracker from the Omega stronghold, uncovers a threat that could spell the end for their fragile society. With friends and enemies revealing truths about the past, she will need to decide who to trust.

Available on Amazon.

DEAD ISLAND: OPERATION ZULU

ALLEN GAMBOA

Ten years after the world was nearly brought to its knees by a zombie Armageddon, there is a race for the antidote! On a remote Caribbean island, surrounded by a horde of hungry living dead, a team of American and Australian commandos must rescue the Antidotes' scientist. Filled with zombies, guns, Russian bad guys, shady government types, serial killers and elevator muzak. Dead Island is an action packed blood soaked horror adventure.

INVASION OF THE DEAD SERIES

OWEN BAILLIE

This is the first book in a series of nine, about an ordinary bunch of friends, and their plight to survive an apocalypse in Australia. -- Deep beneath defense headquarters in the Australian Capital Territory, the last ranking Army chief and a brilliant scientist struggle with answers to the collapse of the world, and the aftermath of an unprecedented virus. Is it a natural mutation, or does the infection contain -- more sinister roots? -- One hundred and fifty miles away, five friends returning from a month-long camping trip slowly discover that death has swept through the country. What greets them in a gradual revelation is an enemy beyond compare. -- Armed with dwindling ammunition, the friends must overcome their disagreements, utilize their individual skills, and face unimaginable horrors as they battle to reach their hometown...

THE GATHERING HORDE

RICH BAKER

The most ambitious terrorist plot ever undertaken is about to be put into motion, releasing an unstoppable force against humanity. Ordinary people – A group of students celebrating the end of the semester, suburban and rural families – are about to themselves in the center of something that threatens the survival of the human species. As they battle the dead – and the living – it's going to take every bit of skill, knowledge and luck for them to survive in Zed's World.

HUMAN ELEMENT

A.J POWERS

They said the Neuroweb would change the world…They had no idea how right they were.

After wandering around the desolate suburbs of Cincinnati for nearly a year, Aaran has legitimate reason to believe he is the last free-thinking human alive. It has been months since he has interacted with someone who wasn't trying to kill or convert him, and the growing agony of nomadic isolation is taking a toll on his already weary mind.

After a close call with a Sentinel—an AI-controlled soldier for the Nebula—Aaran unexpectedly finds himself in the company of Hadas, a beautiful yet dangerous woman. A shaky alliance is formed between the two as they fight to survive. Together, they search for answers to keep them going in such a godforsaken world.

THIS BOOK WAS FORMATTED BY

CARLSINCLAIR.NET

Made in the USA
Las Vegas, NV
03 May 2024

89485829R00177